THE FOURTH WALL
SYNDROME

MARTIN GUNN

Grosvenor House
Publishing Limited

The right of Martin Gunn to be identified as the author of this
work has been asserted in accordance with Section 78
of the Copyright, Designs and Patents Act 1988

The book cover picture is copyright to Martin Gunn

This book is published by
Grosvenor House Publishing Ltd
28-30 High Street, Guildford, Surrey, GU1 3EL.
www.grosvenorhousepublishing.co.uk

A CIP record for this book
is available from the British Library

ISBN 978-1-78148-394-7

To
Carole and Aimee
The loves of my life

Contents

Lives of great men all remind us
We can make our lives sublime
And departing leave behind us
Footprints in the sands of time

A Psalm of Life
Henry Wadsworth Longfellow

PART ONE

THE CONCLAVE

Prologue

Doctor Barnabus Middlebrook ran up the stairs of St. Clare's Psychiatric hospital; he was twenty minutes late for what was almost certainly one of the most important moments in his life. Near the top he tripped on a step and the sets of three folders under his right arm flew across the landing. Cursing to himself he hurriedly collected them together. This was the second time that morning he was picking them up off the floor. Placing them in alphabetical order, he smiled inwardly at the OCD implications of his actions, then frowned as he felt the unfamiliar texture of the smaller boxier Document C. Taking a deep breath he made his way down the long corridor that led to the boardroom. He detested this part of the hospital. It was modern and characterless, part of an extension to St. Clare's that was added in the early 1960's. The addition was completely out of character with the hospital's Victorian looking edifice. The older part of the building was actually completed in 1905, originally as a sanatorium for Tuberculosis sufferers, and then later to help soldiers returning from the Great War that were suffering from shell shock. It was from here on that St. Clare's developed its reputation as a psychiatric hospital and Dr Middlebrook was pre-eminent in this field. Relying heavily on his reputation to arrange this meeting, he suddenly felt nervous, there was a lot at stake, least of all his reputation. Being well aware that his findings may well be construed as risible, even by the most open-minded person, and ridicule could prove a disaster at this juncture, what was needed was a leap of faith. It was a great deal to ask of anyone and he knew it.

Gingerly Dr Middlebrook opened the door to the boardroom, and as he entered, immediately saw the look of disapproval on the face of Dr Anna Rathburn, Chief Executive of St. Clare's. She was wearing a dark grey skirt with matching jacket and white blouse. Minimal make-up and her dark hair tied back in a bun seemed to detract from an attractive face. The overall impression was of a school mistress, her intention being to look as businesslike as possible in an environment dominated by men. At thirty-two, her climb up the career ladder had been swift and Dr Rathburn was reluctant to put it in jeopardy.

"Barny you're late," she hissed, approaching and eying him up and down.

Dr Middlebrook was wearing his usual tatty corduroy jacket and faded jeans. His tie was loose and dishevelled from the recent fall. She noticed that he was red in the face and looked flustered. This was not typical behaviour for him and it made her curious as to why. Middlebrook hated being called Barny and only tolerated it from Dr Rathburn.

"I'm sorry," he gasped in a hushed tone, "something came up – it couldn't wait – it was unavoidable."

"You could have at least made an effort," she admonished. "I assume you want to make a good impression."

Dr Middlebrook just stared at her blankly not knowing how to respond. Sartorial elegance was always low on his priorities. Her comment seemed irrelevant to him.

Dr Rathburn gave in; she knew what he was like. After all, they had known each other for years. When they were younger there had been an unspoken attraction between them, but now it was more of a comfortable friendship. Dr Middlebrook knew that she had pulled strings to set up this meeting as a result of their friendship and wouldn't have done it for anyone else. Her trust in his judgement deserved his appreciation.

"Thanks for doing this, I owe you one."

"It had better be worth it," said Dr Rathburn somewhat harshly, looking for reassurance.

"Oh it's worth it," stated Dr Middlebrook trying to sound more confident than he felt.

Her annoyance subsided. "Tea or coffee?" she sighed in defeat.

"Coffee please," replied Dr Middlebrook, who had just noticed the other three men standing at the end of the boardroom with cups in their hands. They had stopped their small talk and were now staring, curiously in Middlebrook's direction. After being handed a cup of coffee he turned to address the distinguished looking men who were now frowning dubiously.

Well aware that he had not made a good first impression, Middlebrook made his way down the room to introduce himself, it was time to get businesslike.

"Gentlemen," he said with a smile. "My apologies for keeping you waiting but now we are all here shall we sit down, I'm sure you are all busy men and there is a lot to get through."

Everyone took their places: Dr Rathburn at the head of the table and Dr Middlebrook to the side.

Opposite him sat the three men, all cabinet ministers. To his left sat Sir Edmund Wakefield – Secretary of State for the Home Department. In the middle sat Andrew Ballentine – Secretary of State for Defence, and finally sitting on his right was Hector Gerrard – Secretary of State for Health.

They were an intimidating sight; then it suddenly occurred to Dr Middlebrook that they resembled the three wise monkeys. Stifling a laugh, he busied himself passing out the various documents that he had brought with him.

They all looked at Dr Middlebrook doubtfully; this was going to be a complete waste of time.

"Isn't anybody going to take minutes of this meeting?" declared Gerrard.

In his late forties he was the youngest of the three, and since he knew many of the senior staff at St. Clare's, felt that he could assert his authority.

"Absolutely not," insisted Dr Middlebrook. "Everything that is said here today must be kept confidential, so the fewer people who know the better."

"Well," replied Gerrard somewhat pompously, "I find this all very irregular."

"Are all three of us really necessary?" enquired Ballentine, in a tired, rather bored voice. He was in his mid-sixties and the eldest of the three. He made it clear that he would rather be somewhere else.

"Look!" exclaimed Middlebrook showing his irritation, "I would have requested the Prime Minister – if he had been available."

They all raised their eyebrows at this, even Dr Rathburn. She was beginning to wonder whether this was a good idea. With the meeting in danger of being derailed before it got going, Dr Middlebrook breathed in and gathered himself together.

"Okay let's get started," he said in a calmer voice. "In front of you are three files, first we are going to look at the one marked A."

Everyone pulled Document A in front of them and turned to the first page.

CHAPTER ONE
Document A
ALICE'S CONDITION

The first thing that everyone noticed was the six inch by eight inch colour photograph of a young woman paper clipped to the first page. She was attractive in a girl-next-door kind of way, with fair to mousy coloured hair draped just below her shoulders. Her smile suggested someone who was relaxed and happy.

"Pretty girl," said Edmund Wakefield, who was aware that he had not spoken since they had sat down.

"Indeed, but if you look at the photo underneath, you will see how she looks now."

Everyone lifted the top photo to reveal another photograph showing the same girl looking very different. Again in colour, this photo showed a woman who looked much older. Her hair was lank and unkempt, with a down turned mouth; the smile was gone and her eyelids were half closed. Dark rings under her eyes were accentuated by the pallor of her skin.

"The first photo was taken this springtime and the second one, three weeks ago," said Middlebrook, observing the look of shock of those around the table.

"My God, what happened to her?" asked Gerrard.

"That is what we are here to discuss," said Middlebrook, starting to relax a little now he had the three men's attention. Middlebrook continued, "The subject in front of you is Alice Denham. She will be twenty-seven on the eighth of October and is married to John Denham. They have been happily married, at least until recently, for three years. Her demeanour was generally of a happy girl, with a tendency to be shy rather than outgoing. A little highly strung at times perhaps but nothing of any real consequence."

"So she has not shown any psychotic symptoms up until recently?" interjected Dr Rathburn.

"That is correct."

"What are her symptoms?" asked Wakefield.

"I was about to come to that," replied Middlebrook. "When she was first admitted to St. Clare's, Alice exhibited regular bouts of hysteria and paranoia which we have tried to suppress with antipsychotic drugs with some success. She keeps to herself and spends her time listening to her MP3 player or reading. At regular intervals however, she will stop whatever it is she is doing and pace the perimeter of the room, carefully and methodically inspecting the walls. When she is satisfied all is well Alice will then continue with whatever it is she is doing. It is also worth noting that Alice will not tolerate a mirror or any reflective surfaces in her room. As a consequence there is no television, and a blind covers her window when it gets dark." Again eyebrows were raised.

"What on earth is she checking for?" asked an incredulous Wakefield.

"We'll come to that later." Middlebrook didn't want to get ahead of himself at this point.

"Does Alice have a room to herself?" enquired Ballentine.

"Yes she does," stated Middlebrook. "In fact," he continued, "Alice will only tolerate a few people in her room. People she trusts."

"And they are?" enquired Ballentine again.

"Staff Nurse Susan Griffiths and well ... me basically, and that's it," said Middlebrook resignedly.

"However, her room is left unlocked so she is at liberty to leave it at any time and relax in the communal areas but she chooses and indeed prefers not to. She is not considered a threat despite all that has happened."

"And what about her husband?" asked Gerrard. "Will she see him?"

"Absolutely not," uttered Middlebrook excitedly. "When a visit from her husband is suggested Alice starts to get agitated and needs to be calmed. He hasn't once visited St. Clare's or enquired as to her condition. I don't think it's because he does not want to, more that the whole episode has troubled him deeply. I believe he is seeking counselling as well as medical care."

The room fell silent at this point and Middlebrook took the opportunity to continue. "I must stress however that since Alice has been settled here she has improved. She is lucid, coherent and mostly rational, only becoming irrational and sometimes hysterical if you mention her recent experiences."

Middlebrook paused slightly for maximum effect, "Experiences which I call 'The Fourth Wall Syndrome.'"

"What were her recent experiences? And what on earth is the 'Fourth Wall Syndrome'?" enquired Wakefield, before anyone else could get the question out.

"That leads us neatly on to Document B," replied Middlebrook with a faint whiff of smugness in his voice. He knew that he had them hooked. They all pulled Document B towards them and opened the cover. Middlebrook continued. "It all started back in July of this year…"

CHAPTER TWO
Document B
ALICE'S STORY

It was one of those warm summer mornings in mid-July. A day you just knew would be blisteringly hot by mid-afternoon. With a tranquil cloudless sky, nobody could have the Monday morning blues on a day like this, and that's just how Alice Denham felt as she pulled into the drive of her home. She smiled unconsciously as she did so, having moved out of the pokey one bedroom flat just under a year ago which she had shared with her husband John. Despite the fact however that their new home was a fairly nondescript semi-detached, they didn't care; it was theirs, and that's all that mattered.

John and Alice had been married for a little over three years and life couldn't be better: they had their new home; both were in employment with John working in the planning department of the local council, and Alice working as a secretary for a firm of solicitors. The couple were devoted to each other. Alice especially couldn't believe her luck, sometimes feeling that John could have done much better for himself. He was tall, slim with dark well-groomed hair and at certain angles had a hint of George Clooney about him. At least that's what Alice thought.

Having secretly taken the day off, Alice, just returning from the doctors, had another reason to be happy. After months of trying for a baby she could finally tell John that she was pregnant.

The rest of the day went painfully slowly for Alice. After lunch she headed for the supermarket and bought groceries to cook a special meal and a bottle of champagne to celebrate her news. By mid-afternoon she was back home feeling hot and lethargic so decided to take a short nap. John wouldn't be home until 6.00pm so there was plenty of time to get started on the cooking.

John, ever a creature of habit, put his key in the door at three minutes past six and assuming that she had put her car in the garage shouted, "Hi love! Are you in?"

"Where else would I be?" retorted Alice rhetorically, walking out of the kitchen to greet him with a big smile on her face. They kissed and hugged by the doorway and at that moment John, looking over her shoulder, noticed the dining table neatly laid for dinner.

"The table looks nice," he said, suddenly panicking, thinking that he had forgotten some anniversary.

"I just thought that I would make an effort today," said Alice in a teasing tone. "You've got half an hour till dinners ready," she continued.

"Great," said John, "I'm starving, I'll have a quick shower first though, it was sweaty as hell at the office today."

"Yes I noticed!" smiled Alice but John didn't hear, he was already in the bathroom getting undressed.

Twenty minutes later, John walked into the kitchen refreshed and changed, to see Alice standing by the dining table with a glass of champagne in her hand. Again alarm bells went off in his head. What on earth had he forgotten this time? The only thing to do he thought was to bluff it out.

"What's the occasion?" he asked tentatively.

Alice grinned and while handing him the glass picked another one up for herself.

"What are we toasting?" enquired John.

"To us!" replied Alice and then after a short pause, "the three of us!"

John frowned for a second and Alice watched as the information sank in, relishing the moment.

"You mean..." stumbled John.

"Yes!" interrupted Alice no longer able to contain herself. "I'm pregnant!"

"Sweetheart, that's brilliant," He was both excited and relieved knowing just how much this meant, especially to Alice. "How far gone are you?"

"Six weeks," replied Alice. "I checked myself with one of those pregnancy testers on Friday and went to the doctor's this morning to get it confirmed. I needed to register for all that prenatal stuff too."

"Oh my God, I'm going to be a Dad!" he exclaimed, sitting down at the table and taking a large swig of champagne.

"You had better get used to the idea, this one's just the first," chuckled Alice. Soon they were sitting down to eat with the conversation being mostly about babies and the future.

After dinner, Alice started to clear the table and John poured the last drops of champagne into his glass. Having drunk most of the bottle, he was starting to feel a little tipsy since Alice had barely touched any.

"We'd better break the news to our parents," said John walking into the living room to sit down.

"Why don't we have them over for dinner and tell them all together," suggested Alice.

"Makes sense, any thoughts on when?"

"How about this Wednesday?" said Alice, walking into the living room, sitting on John's lap and putting her arm around his shoulder.

"It's not too soon?" ventured John doubtfully.

"I don't think so. I can leave work early to prepare everything," then added, "I'll do a roast. You know how boring our parents can be when it comes to food."

"Fair enough, as long as you are sure," he conceded.

* * *

Tuesday dragged by for Alice, she couldn't wait to break the news to her parents. Ever since they had moved into the new house John's parents in particular had been hinting at when they were going to start a family. During work she planned the following night's meal and straight after work went to the supermarket to get the groceries.

Dinner was arranged for seven o'clock on Wednesday evening. John's parents predictably arrived early and Alice's parents arrived slightly late. The bell rang and Alice opened the door to her mum and dad.

"You're late," she admonished, trying not to sound too harsh. "John's mum and dad have been here for half an hour."

It had been particularly awkward. John's parents were no fools, they knew that something was going on and they didn't want to break the news until both sets of parents were present. Being late didn't help matters.

"Blame your dad," retorted Alice's mum stepping past her, "he's a nightmare to get out of the house these days."

Alice's dad just rolled his eyes and said, "Hello Poppet, I knew it would be my fault." As he walked past her he gave Alice a peck on the cheek.

"Everyone's in the lounge," said Alice over her shoulder and then she closed the door.

The evening went convivially and predictably with both sets of parents being overjoyed at John and Alice's news. With the two of them being only children, the parents knew that they were their only shot at being grandparents; something that John and Alice had both been fully aware of.

Around ten thirty the evening was over, John walked his parents to the front door to see them off while Alice went into the living room to start clearing up. She bent down to pick up the glasses from the coffee table placing them on a tray. Then as she stood up again holding the tray she happened to glance at her reflection in the mirror over the fireplace. But instead of seeing the wall on the opposite side of the room, she saw rows of strange creatures seated and staring at her. It was as if they were in another room but the wall had been removed. She screamed and dropped the tray swinging round to look at the back wall. The image reflected in the mirror was not there and all she could see was the wall. Instantly Alice turned back to the mirror again but all was normal. The strange apparition was gone.

Hearing the scream and the sound of a tray hitting the floor, John dashed into the living room to see a visibly shaken Alice about to bend down to pick up the broken glass.

"What happened?"

"I don't know," trembled Alice on the verge of tears.

"Come on, leave that to me. You go up," said John, "you must be tired. I'll clear up here."

"Don't be long," she whimpered, wiping a tear from her face.

"Of course not," he said comfortingly.

As Alice turned and walked out of the room John couldn't help but notice the look of fear in her expression.

Shortly after, John entered the bedroom to see Alice already tucked up in bed. Despite the fact that it was another hot night she had pulled the duvet fully over her shoulders. He got undressed and slipped in beside her, putting his arm out inviting Alice to snuggle into him. She responded and held him tight.

"Are you okay?" John asked softly, with more than a little concern.

"Yes," she replied simply – but it was a lie, she was far from okay.

As John fell into a deep sleep Alice lay there holding him, going over in her head what had happened in the living room. She must have been seeing things surely? And the creatures, they looked so alien with large black almond shaped eyes and high foreheads. The whole incident kept running over in her mind until eventually she fell into a troubled unsettled sleep.

* * *

Thursday dawned to another warm and sunny day, though Alice did not see it. John awoke to see Alice fully dressed at the window staring, seemingly blankly at the blue cloudless sky.

"Good morning sweetheart," he greeted, rubbing his eyes, "sleep okay?"

Alice turned and gave him a weak smile, "not too bad, I've finished in the bathroom if you want to use it. I'll start breakfast."

Alice made her way downstairs and John went to the bathroom. The first thing that he noticed was a towel which Alice had obviously draped over the mirror. He frowned at this odd behaviour and took the towel down so that he could shave. When he came down to the kitchen he saw that Alice had made toast and coffee. He decided to overlook the incident with the towel and sat down to eat. The conversation during breakfast was somewhat muted and soon both of them were heading out of the door to work.

With her job taking her mind off things, Alice started to feel a little brighter; something that John noticed when he got home that evening. Perhaps it's her hormones he thought, not really knowing what attributed to her mood.

By the end of office hours on Friday, Alice was more or less back to normal and looking forward to the weekend with John. It had become a tradition on Friday nights to have a takeaway, and at 6.30 John left the house to pick up a pizza.

After doing some tidying up in the kitchen Alice walked into the living room. Inadvertently she again caught her reflection in the mirror over the fireplace. Then it happened just as before. Rows of strange alien-looking creatures were staring at her, as if from a secret room. She felt a hot flush of panic rise up her body and she instinctively swung round to look at the wall. This time however the apparition was there for her to see. Just for a few seconds the image remained. Enough time for her to see the look of surprise on some of the faces staring back at her. Suddenly the vision faded to the familiar patterned wallpaper at a speed that caused her to blink and refocus her eyes.

Alice gave a prolonged gasp seemingly unable to scream. Then on the verge of a panic attack and breathing heavily, she ran into the kitchen, opened the door to the garden and ran blindly to the bottom trying to hide behind the thin trunk of a cherry tree. Her mind was racing, she couldn't think straight. What the hell was going on? Was she going mad? She looked at the house – all looked normal – and, still breathing erratically, she turned round with her back to the tree trunk, slid down and started sobbing.

Half an hour later, John entered the house and called to Alice but got no answer; the house appeared to be empty. After checking the living room where he had left her, John walked into the kitchen to see the door into the rear garden wide open. Frowning, he placed the pizza on the kitchen table and walked to the door. Initially the garden looked empty until eventually he spied Alice huddled behind the cherry tree.

"Alice," he called, but didn't get a response. He hurried to the tree to find Alice sat there with her knees pulled up towards her and her head buried in her hands sobbing uncontrollably.

"Alice – sweetheart what is it?" Before she could reply he knelt down and put his arms around her. Still sobbing Alice wrapped her arms around John so tightly she was almost strangling him.

"Don't make me go back into the house," cried Alice between sobs.

"What's wrong?" replied John perplexed. "What has upset you?"

Alice didn't reply but continued to hold him tightly. Gradually her laboured breathing subsided and she looked him in the eyes and said, "They're watching me."

"Who – who's watching you?" John was even more confused now.

"I see them – they're watching me ... and you. They're watching the house."

"Who are? This is crazy come back inside and we'll talk about it."

Alice panicked and pushed him away. "No – please I ... I can't," she said, shaking her head vigorously. Her eyes were wide with a look of sheer terror.

John was perplexed. He couldn't force her back inside. He thought for a few moments then said softly, "I'm going to phone your mum." Alice made no response and John walked back to the house to find his mobile. Soon he was explaining the situation to Alice's mother, Janet. Clearly concerned she put the phone down and got straight into her car to come over.

In less than ten minutes, she had pulled up outside the house and was ringing the doorbell. John opened the door and before he could greet Jane, she said, "Is she still down there?" then walked past him into the hallway, through the kitchen and out into the garden. John barely had a chance to nod a reply but walked to the kitchen door to see what was happening. Alice's mother started talking to her daughter; Alice seemed to reply and then they hugged. Alice's mother spoke again and at this point John wished that he could lip read as he couldn't hear either of them.

Eventually they were heading back towards the house with Alice's mother holding her close as they walked. As they got near the house Alice started getting agitated. John walked towards them.

"She won't come inside John so I am going to take her home with me tonight," said Janet.

She passed her car keys to John and said, "Take Alice to my car while I go and pack an overnight bag."

"Okay you'll find a weekend bag under the bed." replied John, finding himself somewhat relieved – a wave of guilt rushing through him for feeling that way. Janet noticed his unease and putting a hand on his arm to reassure him said, "It'll be alright John. I know it's easier said than done, but try not to worry."

John walked with Alice down the path by the side of the garage that led to the front of the house, whilst Janet walked into the kitchen and made her way up the stairs. The first thing she did was to take Alice's pink toothbrush from the bathroom and then entered the bedroom. With the bag retrieved from under the bed, Janet selected a few items of clothing from the wardrobe and then moved over to Alice's bedside unit to get some underwear. She pulled open the top drawer and was surprised to see an eight inch kitchen knife laying on top. She picked up the knife and stared at it. What on earth was it doing there? Who was she afraid of? Was it John? Surely not. After taking some under garments she placed the knife back in the drawer and decided to say nothing. At least for the time being.

As she approached the car, Janet took the keys from John and said, "I'll ring you tomorrow," then walked round to the driver's side of the car.

"I'll speak to you tomorrow sweetheart," said John reassuringly to Alice.

With the car door closed and the window fully up, Alice just gave him a withering smile. John watched as the car pulled away and drove out of sight. Then he walked forlornly back up the drive.

* * *

John got up late on Saturday morning and decided that despite everything that had happened he was going to the club to play rugby as he always did. He felt guilty for doing it and for not ringing, but damn it he needed a break and Alice was in safe hands after all.

After the match the team had showered and were getting dressed. John's close friend Colin had noticed a change in him. He seemed preoccupied, withdrawn and reticent.

"Are you okay?" queried Colin. "You don't seem your usual jovial self, old chap."

John was unsure how to reply; he couldn't say that Alice was slowly going out of her brain even if he did think so himself. Finally he said, "Yeah I'm okay – I've just got some shit happening at the moment." John left it at that and Colin sensed not to press the subject any further. As they both were about to leave, Colin said, "Are you still up for a drink on Tuesday?"

"I hope so, I'll ring you to confirm."

Walking to his car, John pulled out his mobile phone and switched it on. To his surprise he had a dozen messages on it, all from Janet. He slid into the driver's seat and rang her.

Janet answered and John said, "Hi – is Alice okay? What's happened?"

Janet sounded flustered. "She has gone home."

"What? – When?" said John starting to get flustered himself.

"About two hours ago. I have been trying to get hold of you. Where have you been for God's sake?"

John ignored the question, his mind was racing. "Why didn't you stop her, I was about to come round?"

"And how am I supposed to do that. She's a grown woman, I couldn't stop her."

Janet calmed herself down a little to say, "She was rambling about refusing to be forced out of her own home by peeping Toms or something."

"I'd better get home," said John with some urgency.

"She would have been home for a while now," said Janet then added, "oh and before I forget, I managed to get her an appointment at the doctor's for Monday at 10.30. Luckily they had a cancellation."

"Okay," said John, "I'll take her myself and make sure she keeps the appointment."

During the drive home John couldn't help but feel some slight resentment towards Janet for calling the doctor's surgery without consulting him first but had to concede it was the right thing to do. Putting his key in the front door it suddenly occurred to John that Alice hadn't taken a key with her; or so he thought. He opened the door and called, "Alice, are you here?"

There was no reply but as he walked into the hallway John could hear activity in the kitchen. He walked in and saw Alice placing all the mirrors in the house on the kitchen table. Then he noticed the broken window in the kitchen door.

"What's going on?" he enquired.

"The mirrors – must get rid of the mirrors," mumbled Alice in a monotone voice and without looking up, "the mirrors are the problem."

"You've smashed the window – you could have cut yourself," replied a concerned John. Walking to the table he tried to pick up one of the mirrors whilst saying, "This is ridiculous let's…" But before he could finish the sentence Alice lunged and pushed him with a force that he didn't expect. Caught off balance he stumbled back.

"No!" screamed Alice at the top of her voice, "Leave them – they must go." Then in a whisper, "They must go."

"Hey it's alright," soothed John, putting his arm around her. He felt her body grow tense with the physical contact. "Look," he said, trying to ignore it, "why don't we just put them all in the cupboard under the stairs eh?"

Alice nodded with uncertainty and watched him as he picked up all the mirrors that Alice had collected from around the house, and put them in the under-stairs cupboard.

"There," he said, "done."

Alice just gave him a blank look and walked past on her way to the bedroom.

After fitting a wooden board to secure the kitchen door, John cooked a meal which he ate alone in front of the television, hoping it would take his mind off of the predicament, but found it difficult to concentrate.

In the bedroom, Alice sat cross legged on the bed picking at her food and staring blankly at the wall.

* * *

Sunday morning John awoke in the spare bedroom. The night before, he decided to give Alice some space. Plus he felt like he needed a good night's sleep himself. He got up and looked in on Alice. She was still fast asleep so he decided to make some toast and coffee and bring it up to the bedroom. Shortly John opened the bedroom door to see Alice stirring.

"Morning sweetheart," he said cheerily, trying to keep her spirits up. He noticed with a frown of concern that she had hardly touched her food from the night before. "I've brought some breakfast up," he said, placing the tray on the bed, "you hardly touched your food from last night – am I that bad a cook?" he joked trying to keep the mood light.

Alice gave him a weak smile and simply said, "I wasn't hungry – sorry."

"Look," said John, "why don't we get out today. Go for a walk down at the park and then grab a bite to eat at a pub?"

The prospect of getting out of the house perked Alice up a little and by late morning they were strolling through the park in the summer sunshine. They walked through a small wooded area where shafts of sunlight were piercing through the branches. They were holding hands and for now at least it seemed as though everything was normal. Presently the trees opened up to a lake and they could see people feeding ducks. John steered them towards the lake but about twenty feet away from the edge, Alice stopped dead whilst John walked on.

"You will have to get a bit closer," he said with a big smile, "if you want to see the ducks."

Alice shook her head, "No," she said nervously.

John frowned, "What is it?" he said perplexed at her reaction.

"Reflections," retorted Alice, "I don't like reflections."

With the carefree moment lost, John put his arm around her and said, "Okay – let's find a nice pub with a garden." Alice nodded and they headed back to the car.

After a pleasant lunch in a country pub they took a scenic route home and arrived back by late afternoon. It had been a relaxing day but now John noticed Alice becoming tense again as they entered the house.

"Come on," he said reassuringly, "let's watch some telly, there's bound to be a film on."

They walked into the living room; John first then Alice, very tentatively following behind him.

"Come in," he said, "it's fine."

Alice finally entered the room and soon they were both sitting on the sofa watching television.

Around 7.00pm Alice got up and said, "Fancy a cuppa?"

"Yes great idea," enthused John, encouraged by her improvement. "How about some biscuits too," he added.

"Aren't you still full from lunch?" she said incredulously.

"I've always got room for a choky biscuit."

Alice smiled and padded off to the kitchen.

John breathed a sigh of relief; it seemed as though Alice was slowly getting back to her old self.

Ten minutes later, she entered the room with a tray in her hands and as she turned to place it on the coffee table, there was a sudden flash of light and the wall opposite the mantelpiece was completely gone. Alice dropped the tray, she could see in front of her rows of alien looking creatures, as many as fifty, all seated and looking at her as though they were an audience. The creatures all looked similar. High foreheads, large black almond shaped eyes and wearing similar shiny black suits. Their skin was flesh coloured with a faint hint of grey.

She just stood there staring, eyes wide in terror mouth wide open making a strange gurgling sound like a scream caught in her throat. The picture hanging on the wall of her and John on their wedding day seemed to be floating in mid-air. Most of the creatures started to frown, as if they too were perplexed at what was happening. Some had started to get up and talk, moving slowly to where the wall should have been.

Alice recoiled and started screaming. Still transfixed by the vision, she backed into an armchair and stepped onto it, trying to get as far away as possible. Not only could she see them but now, she could faintly hear them too.

John jumped up and ran to her. "What is it for God's sake!" he exclaimed. He was panicking and didn't know why.

Alice was hysterical now, struggling to speak. "The wall," she screamed eventually, pointing at it. "Can't you see, I can hear them now," her eyes tightly shut and her hands over her ears.

John looked at the wall still perplexed and said, "I can't see anything – there's nothing there."

By now the creatures were getting closer to the invisible wall and Alice in a fit of panic pushed past John and ran out of the room and up the stairs into the bedroom. He heard the bedroom door slam shut as he sat there dumbfounded for a moment staring at the offending wall. After a short while he stood up, walked to the wall and ran his hands over it. It seemed perfectly normal to him. Solid! He looked back to where Alice had just run out of the room and said to himself: "It's just a wall for fuck's sake."

After what seemed an age, John made his way up to the bedroom to find Alice huddled in a corner, still and silent. As the door opened she flinched for a second until she realised it was John.

"Don't let them get me," she whispered in a tearful quivering voice.

"Who? there's no one there."

"The aliens," she continued, "they want me."

"Let's get you into bed," soothed John.

Initially Alice resisted and then gave up and allowed John to manoeuvre her onto the bed. John slipped into the bed and he hugged her tightly. And that's how they stayed until morning with John getting hardly any sleep.

* * *

The waiting room of the doctor's surgery was packed on Monday morning when John and Alice arrived at 10.20. Janet had done well to get them an appointment. They managed to get the last seats and waited patiently in silence until the doctor called them in. Alice sat there and gently rocked back and forth completely consumed with her own thoughts, seemingly oblivious to her present surroundings. A few people sitting opposite her noticed and watched curiously, until they were called in for their appointment.

John was surprised they had managed to get there at all, let alone be ten minutes early. Motivating Alice that morning had been an uphill struggle. She hadn't wanted to get out of bed, had to be forced to wash and get dressed and wouldn't eat any breakfast. John finally managed to get her to drink a cup of tea, and all this was done with Alice barely uttering a word.

Finally, after a half hour wait, they were called in by the doctor. John guided Alice into the room as if she had no will of her own and sat her down. He then pulled up a spare chair and sat down next to her.

"What seems to be the problem?" enquired the doctor.

"It's my wife, Alice, she seems to be having some sort of a breakdown."

The doctor scanned over Alice's notes on his computer. Remembering her from the previous week he noticed a significant change in her physical appearance and general demeanour.

"Ah yes, I thought so," he said, thinking out loud, "you came in last week to confirm your pregnancy."

Alice just stared blankly back at him and made no reply.

"What happened?" enquired the doctor.

"She claims to be seeing things at home – hallucinating. She says they are trying to get her," John felt very uncomfortable discussing it.

"Has Alice told you what she is seeing?" asked the doctor.

"Yes – she has mentioned 'aliens' a few times." When John mentioned aliens Alice suddenly started to become very agitated and needed calming down.

"Don't upset yourself my dear," said the doctor kindly, "what is this nonsense?"

Alice started rocking back and forth in the chair again, making a moaning sound. Clearly she was very disturbed.

The doctor thought for a minute and then said, "Will you excuse me a minute," and he left the room. They sat silently in the surgery and John placed his hand in Alice's, who squeezed it very tightly. When the doctor returned, he sat down and turned to them.

"I think Alice will benefit from seeing a psychiatrist. I have set up an appointment with a Dr Brocklehurst for this Thursday afternoon at 2.30. I trust you can make it?" he said, looking at John and handing him the address.

"Of course, I'll see that she gets there," John replied bluntly.

"In the meantime," continued the doctor, "I am going to prescribe Diazepam to help Alice sleep at night. She looks exhausted. Take no more than one before bedtime. Is that clear?" the doctor continued, "it's not ideal giving a pregnant woman sedatives but I am more concerned about your wife's obvious distress and the effect that that might have on the baby. Hopefully it will only be for a few days."

John nodded, thanked the doctor and helped Alice to the door. Just as John was about to close the door, he turned and asked, "Do you think the pregnancy could have caused this?"

The doctor thought for a second and then replied, "It's possible, though I personally haven't seen anything so severe as this. Hopefully Dr Brocklehurst will be able to get to the bottom of it." He smiled kindly and John closed the door and left.

Soon they were back home and Alice went straight back up to the bedroom. John decided to give Alice one tablet which he obtained from the surgery pharmacy and then made a few phone calls. First he phoned Janet to bring her up to speed, and then realising he hadn't informed his own parents of recent events, phoned them next. Finally, he phoned his friend Colin to confirm that he would be down the pub at around eight the following evening.

* * *

After several days without shaving, John noticed his stubble was starting to irritate. So before going down to meet Colin for a drink he decided to retrieve the bathroom mirror from under the stairs. Carefully he slid it out from underneath the other mirrors so as not to disturb Alice who was sleeping in the bedroom. Then he took it up to the bathroom and hung it over the sink. Feeling better after a shower and shave, John got dressed and kissed the still sleeping Alice gently on the cheek. She didn't stir so John left to make his way to the pub.

When he arrived half an hour late, Colin was propping up the bar with an almost empty glass of beer in his hand.

"John," he greeted enthusiastically, "at last, what are you having?"

Immediately he could see that something was wrong, John did not look happy at all. He ordered John a pint and said, "You look like hell, what is it mate?"

God, where do I start, thought John. "It's Alice," replied John eventually, "there's something seriously wrong with her; it came on so suddenly last week."

John went on to tell Colin the whole sorry story, Colin listening intently with fascination.

"So what happened after you got back from the doctor's yesterday?" said Colin.

"Very little actually, we got home; she took a pill and slept. Apart from the odd drink and bite to eat that's how it has been until now. I left her sleeping when I came out tonight."

"Is she safe to leave on her own?" enquired Colin with a concerned frown on his face.

"Well considering she is sleeping most of the time now I should think so," said John, not totally convinced by his reply. Colin wasn't convinced either but just nodded, keeping his opinions to himself. "I needed to get out of the house, just for a while," added John, "but I suppose I'd better start thinking about getting back soon."

Again Colin nodded, he couldn't believe that John had left Alice alone in the first place but who was he to judge. He thought to himself, *it wasn't him that was going through it.*

Just over an hour later John pulled into the drive and as he got out of the car he could see some movement through the window. It was difficult to make out in the half light of dusk so he anxiously put his key in door and stepped in.

Opening the door to the living room, John saw Alice at the wall that she was currently obsessed with. She was in her nightdress, gliding her hands over the wall and muttering to herself.

"Alice," enquired John, "what are you doing?"

Without looking round, her attention fixated on the wall, Alice said, "They called me down, I can hear them now. Can't you?" She turned her head slowly to look at John. Her eyes were wide and wild looking and she had a creepy mirthless grin on her face. It barely looked like Alice at all. "Come and say hello," she said, in a calm but sinister voice, "they want to meet you."

John had his hands to his mouth; a tear ran down his left cheek. This couldn't be happening. All he could see was the wall. For Alice however it was different. Separated by an invisible barrier, several of the alien-like creatures had moved up close to their side of the wall and were acting like they were trying to break through. Slapping their hands against the wall, causing a ripple effect, like a stone thrown into a pond. Clearly they could see and hear what was going on and they started to laugh. Alice turned back to the wall and saw them laughing.

She put her hands up to her face and said, "They're laughing at us now." And as she said it she starting laughing uncontrollably until she became hysterical. Her humourless laughing wouldn't stop and John, no longer able to take anymore shouted, "There's nothing there you mad bitch!"

Alice's laughter stopped instantly and she just stood staring blankly into the room saying nothing, doing nothing.

Walking into the room John, now feeling guilty for his outburst, put an arm around her waist and guided her out into the hallway, giving a backward glance at the wall as he went as if he might suddenly see something. He saw nothing so took Alice upstairs and settled her into bed. Then getting undressed John slipped into bed and started to reach out to Alice. Her back was to him and he stopped, thinking better of it. Instead he turned over and tried to get to sleep, his mind racing. Alice lay there staring into the darkness seemingly catatonic.

Both were eventually sleeping restlessly until the small hours of the morning when Alice started to wake up. She was facing John who was still fast asleep. She blinked and rubbed her eyes and as they became more accustomed to the light she saw an alien face in the bed staring back at her – grinning. Suddenly, she was wide awake and screaming, rapidly backing out of the bed in terror. John woke up with a start. He could see Alice scrambling across the floor. Pushing up on his knees he gestured to Alice to reassure her but all Alice saw was an alien coming towards her. Wedged in a corner by her bedside drawers, Alice was panicking, screaming and inconsolable. John got closer and as he did so Alice scrambled to pull open the top drawer of the unit and grabbed the eight inch kitchen knife and wildly swung it at John. The tip of the blade caught John's left cheek and made a two inch gash. John gave out a gasp of shock but before he was able to react further, Alice plunged the knife with great force into his left shoulder. The knife went in deep and punctured the top edge of his left lung. Winded and gasping, John fell back on the bed in intense pain, the knife still deep in his shoulder. *What was she doing with a knife in the drawer?* he thought. She obviously felt that she needed protection. His breathing became erratic and he could feel the warmth of the blood that had oozed from the cut on his cheek; noticing his pillow turning red.

Alice, still hysterical, stood up and still screaming ran into the bathroom and locked the door. The first thing she saw as she turned around was the mirror over the sink. With a scream that was as much anger as fear she slammed both her fists down onto the mirror so that it shattered and scattered shards of glass all over the bathroom floor.

John, laying on the bed half dazed, heard the noise and said to himself, "Oh God the mirror, I left it in there."

He stumbled to his feet and staggered to the bathroom door. His breathing was becoming laboured as his lung was starting to fill with blood. "Alice, open the door!" he shouted. But there was no reply. He had no choice but to kick open the door.

It finally flew open after three kicks. He grabbed hold of the door frame to support himself. Kicking the door open had been agony and he was starting to feel weak. Alice was slumped on the floor under the sink, she had used a pointed shard of glass to cut deep into her left wrist and blood was pumping out and spraying all over the bathroom. As she was about to try and cut her other wrist, John stepped in and kicked the glass out of her hand. Panicking, he looked around for something to stop the blood flow and pulled the belt out of a bath robe hanging on the back of the bathroom door. He then tied a knot in the middle of it. John placed the knot over the wound and wrapped the rest of the belt around Alice's wrist tightly. The flow of blood was stemmed but started to soak rapidly into the towelling. John knew that he would have to find a better solution then remembered he had a roll of adhesive tape in his bedside drawer. Picking up his mobile phone at the same time, he staggered back into the bathroom, removed the belt and quickly started wrapping the tape around the wound until the blood stopped. He looked around the bathroom; there was blood up the walls, on the ceiling over the floor, and a small pool of blood had collected in Alice's lap. Shards of glass lay everywhere and John cursed himself for his stupidity.

Alice gave out a faint groan, she was almost unconscious. John slumped back against the wall opposite her, blood from the knife wound was running down his chest. He put his right hand up to the handle with thoughts of pulling it out but gave up as the pain was excruciating and he was fast losing strength. With his head swimming, John picked up his mobile, dialled 999 to call for an ambulance. His right lung was filling with blood and he could barely talk.

"Help – my wife has slashed her wrist and I've been stabbed in the shoulder," he gasped in a burbling voice.

He just managed to give the woman on the other end of the line his address and she said an ambulance and police car will be there as soon as possible. John didn't hear this. He had dropped the phone and had passed out.

* * *

"How did you get our phone numbers?" enquired Mr Denham, John's father.

"We had to break the door down to get in, and I found a phone book in the hallway with your phone numbers in and contacted you straight away," replied WPC Shelby, who was sitting opposite John's mother and father in the hospital family waiting room. Mrs Denham was gently sobbing into a paper handkerchief and trying to control herself, when Janet and her husband came in. Janet was crying also and John's mother stood up to give her a hug.

Feeling guilty, Janet had confessed to her husband that she knew about the knife as they made their way to the hospital. Shocked at his wife's poor judgement he advised that they keep this to themselves.

"What's happening?" said Alice's father.

"We haven't heard anything yet," replied Mr Denham.

"The doctors will be in as soon as there is some news," stated WPC Shelby, trying to sound reassuring.

They all sat down and discussed what they all knew, with WPC Shelby taking notes trying to piece it all together. After what seemed like an eternity a doctor entered the room and sat down with them.

"Hi," he said tying to sound upbeat, "My name is Dr Gilman – I'm sure you're anxious for news on John and Alice." They all nodded expectantly. "Well," he continued, "John is in surgery now but is expected to make a full recovery. He will however be left with a scar on his face from the knife wound."

John's mother gave a gasp and started crying again.

"What about Alice?" "Janet cried, unable to contain herself.

"She is stable now and under sedation in intensive care," replied Dr Gilman.

"What about the baby?" cried Janet again. "Alice is pregnant!"

The doctor shook his head. "I'm sorry," he said, "she just lost too much blood."

Both mothers were crying now and were being consoled by their respective husbands.

Dr Gilman gave his condolences and got up to leave the room. WPC Shelby followed him out and closed the door behind her. "How bad was it?" she asked the doctor, "I haven't seen anything like it."

"It was touch and go for a while – we nearly lost her at one point."

"What will happen now?"

"Well," sighed the doctor, "from what I have heard clearly this is no ordinary domestic. When Alice is strong enough there is a psychoanalyst of some repute that I know, who I'm sure will be interested in this case. It's highly likely that she will need to be sectioned."

* * *

"And that's where I enter the story," said Middlebrook to a somewhat stunned room, "four days later Alice was admitted to St. Clare's. That was six weeks ago and she has been here ever since."

"This is absurd," Ballentine erupted, "clearly the girl is insane and is in exactly the right place." He looked around the room to gauge the reaction of the others. Wakefield nodded and said, "I still don't understand what all this has to do with us."

Ballentine was about to speak again but was cut dead by Gerrard. "What is this wall syndrome thing that you mentioned earlier?" he enquired with genuine interest.

Grateful to Gerrard for getting the meeting back on track, Middlebrook leant back in his chair and said, "Ah yes 'The Fourth Wall Syndrome'. The term the fourth wall was coined in the nineteenth century by a theatre critic I believe. When you watch a play that is set say, in a sitting room, the stage makes up three walls of the room: two walls, one on each side, and the third at the back of the stage. There is also a fourth, invisible wall which separates the actors from the audience. The actors play out their roles seemingly oblivious to the fact that they are being watched by an audience. Very occasionally actors would talk directly to the audience as part of the plot. This technique often used for comic effect is called 'breaking the fourth wall'. It is sometimes used in film and television these days."

"Like the Michael Cain film *Alfie?*" suggested Dr Rathburn.

"Exactly – yes."

"Like a Shakespearian soliloquy then?" offered Wakefield, missing the point.

"No, a soliloquy is generally a lone person on stage thinking out loud," Middlebrook continued, "the character is not talking directly to, and indeed are not aware of the presence of the audience."

Wakefield nodded, satisfied with Middlebrook's reply.

"Like the actors in a story, Alice broke the fourth wall when she had her visions," said Middlebrook.

"Absolutely ridiculous," blustered Ballentine again, "you talk as though you are taking all of this seriously." He looked at everyone around the room expecting them to back him up.

"Do I take this seriously?" replied Middlebrook calmly, "damn right I do, for two reasons. Firstly," he continued, "Alice is not the only one to suffer from this condition. I have had reports of six cases around the world. One in Argentina, one in France, and others spread around Asia. There may be many other cases that haven't been reported that we don't know about."

"Alice isn't a special case then," suggested Gerrard.

"Ah but she is," insisted Middlebrook, "the visions the others had are not as vivid, as real as Alice's, being faint ghost like images, plus she is the only one to hear them. And that makes her unique."

Middlebrook paused to let this sink in.

"And the second reason?" said Ballentine, the cynical tone still in his voice.

"This," insisted Middlebrook, holding up a box about eight inches square and an inch deep. It had a purple metallic look that shimmered with iridescence.

Across the front Middlebrook had stuck a strip of masking tape and in black felt tip pen had written 'Document C'.

CHAPTER THREE
Document C
THE VOICE OF SANITY

The box was passed around the room for closer inspection: first to Dr Rathburn and then the three ministers. They all took it in turns to tilt and turn the box trying to find a way in.

"What is it?" enquired Ballentine, "where did it come from?" He was asking the questions that were on everyone's lips.

"The box is a container," replied Middlebrook, "and it mysteriously turned up in my office two weeks ago. I found it on the floor as I walked in.

Interestingly," he continued, "everything on my desk had been scattered around the room."

Dr Rathburn, knowing the chaotic state of his desk, thought that this might be an improvement, but kept her thoughts to herself. Middlebrook passed the box to Dr Rathburn to inspect, who then duly passed it to Gerrard.

"The material that the box is made from is interesting too," said Middlebrook, "it's cool to the touch and has the strength of a metal but also the flexibility of a plastic. It's neither fish nor fowl."

"How do you open it?" enquired Wakefield, who finally passed the box back to Middlebrook, "I couldn't even find a join."

"Like this," demonstrated Middlebrook. He took the box, and held his finger at a particular spot on the edge. The box opened to reveal a foam-like material with a shiny metal looking object recessed inside. It was about four inches long, one inch wide and about half an inch deep. The edges were rounded and it looked like a silver ingot. They all leant forward to get a closer look.

"How did you know to do that?" asked Gerrard.

"More to the point," ventured Ballentine, "what the hell is it?"

"I ran my finger along its edge trying to find some means of entry, when the box suddenly made a few bleeps and opened," replied Middlebrook. As for what it is," he continued, "it is a storage device."

"So it was activated by your finger print," assumed Gerrard.

"Well, no actually," corrected Middlebrook. "I thought that at first but it seems that my DNA is the only thing that will open the box. It configures itself to the first person to touch it. Since the box was left in my office, I can only assume it was intended that that person be me." Anticipating their next question, he said, "I know this because I took a swab of my saliva and tried it."

To demonstrate he closed the box, took a plastic tube from out of his side pocket removed the long swab stick and ran it along the edge of the box. It opened instantly.

"Good Lord!" exclaimed Wakefield, "extraordinary."

"How do you know that it is a storage device?" enquired Ballentine with genuine interest; his cynicism put to one side.

"I didn't at first, then later that day, I opened my laptop and switched it on. Instantly I heard a faint hum coming from the box. I switched off again and the humming stopped. So I took the device out of the box and placed it next to my laptop and switched back on. To my surprise a video started playing immediately."

He continued talking, lifting his hand up towards them to stave off a barrage of questions. "You all have a transcript of all that is contained here, in Document C in front of you, but I think it's important that you see this."

They all nodded like salivating dogs.

"Anna," said Middlebrook forgetting protocol for a moment, "can I use your laptop?"

Nodding, Dr Rathburn reluctantly slid her laptop over to Middlebrook. She was worried that her files might be corrupted though this was hardly the time to quibble. Sensing her unease Middlebrook said with a reassuring smile, "No need to worry – it won't be harmed."

Middlebrook opened the lid of the laptop, turned it through ninety degrees so that everyone could see the screen, and switched on. He then removed the shiny object from its box and it started to hum, then he placed it next to the laptop.

Immediately the screen sprang into life.

* * *

The first thing they saw was a windowless room, almost empty and about twenty feet square. The floor and walls were an off white colour, lit by a diffused but bright light. In the centre of the room stood a chair, it looked as though it had been carved out of granite, being light grey in colour and with minimal padding. A brighter light from no obvious source shone vertically downwards to highlight the chair.

Suddenly, the screen went black for a few seconds until shards of light began to appear at the edges of the screen. It became apparent that a figure was moving away from a camera and walking towards the chair. From behind, the figure looked tall and slim with short downy white hair on the back of his head. He was wearing a black suit of jacket and trousers and shiny black shoes. The figure turned as he reached the chair and sat down. His head was almost flat on top with the short downy white hair coming to a slight widow's peak in the centre of his forehead. The nose was small and poorly defined, though elongated nostrils were easily discernible, the mouth and lips were wide and thin with only a faint hint of colour in them. His skin was a pale flesh colour with a hint of grey. The most striking thing about his face however was the eyes. Large shiny and jet black, they were the shape of almonds and with a slight tilt downwards towards the bridge of the nose, giving him a sinister look. One could have been forgiven for thinking that he was wearing sun glasses, until he blinked. To each eye it was like two sliding doors meeting in the middle, closing and opening rapidly.

Eventually he smiled and said, "Hello, greetings and salutations." His speech was in perfect English.

Crossing his legs he continued, "My name is Ds Zel-Enni and this message comes to you from a long, long way away. Not in distance you must understand but in time. The future in fact: Earth's future."

Pausing for dramatic effect Zel-Enni went on, "How far into the future we cannot be sure. The time machine that we are developing is very crude at the moment but we are improving it all the time. Our best estimate is that we are around four hundred and seventy thousand years ahead of you. Give or take a few millennia."

Zel-Enni stood up and held his long, lithe arms out horizontally. "Take a good look. Behold the evolution of the human race."

There were gasps around the meeting room and they all looked at each other except for Middlebrook who knew what was coming. Their attention was brought back to the screen as Zel-Enni sat down and started talking again.

"We have been watching you for decades; learning your language, studying your customs. This was all we were able to do for a very long time until recently. Now we are able to send inorganic objects, hence this message. I trust we got the co-ordinates right so as not to cause too much disruption."

"No, of course not," commented Middlebrook sarcastically, "just a large burn mark on the carpet and my office in disarray."

"For some reason, that we do not understand yet," continued Zel-Enni, "we can only lock on to your year and only a small part of it too. Our time is very different to yours. We have achieved things that you could not possibly imagine. All is not well however, we live in troubled times, my people lack empathy and suffer mild psychopathic tendencies." He smiled at the screen. "Consider me the voice of sanity in a world going slowly mad. And speaking of madness, why have you not listened to the girl Alice – though you do seem to have a habit of ignoring your prophets. She is extraordinary and unique. My people are very interested in her."

Zel-Enni leant forward in his seat. "And this brings me to the purpose of this message, it comes by way of a warning: my people intend to invade just as soon as the technology allows. Why am I sending this warning? Well unlike them I see the insanity of it. Prepare yourselves as best you can – war is coming to your time and soon and there is nothing you can do to stop it."

He leant back in his chair with a genuine look of regret then sighed and said, "I will bid you farewell and let's hope that the catastrophic implications of our intentions do not come to pass."

Ds Zel-Enni then lifted his right arm and swung it horizontally to his left. The screen on the lap top suddenly went blank.

Everyone around the room sat in stunned silence. Middlebrook picked up the silver object and placed it back in its box. Then he turned to the three ministers and said in a pompous tone, "Well gentlemen, do you still think Alice is mad?"

Dr Rathburn, sensing that Middlebrook was getting a little confrontational, interjected, "Well it's one o'clock gentlemen; shall we break for lunch. I have arranged for something to be brought in. Excuse me while I go and see if it's ready."

As she got up she cast Middlebrook a glance to show her disapproval. Middlebrook understood and realised that he was going to have to rein himself in.

* * *

As lunch was finishing, Middlebrook pulled out a piece of folded paper from his side pocket, unfolded it and presented the image to the room.

"This rendition was drawn by an artist whilst Alice described them under hypnotherapy some weeks ago."

The picture was passed around the room. It showed an image that looked very similar to Ds Zel-Enni.

"Has Alice seen the video?" asked Ballentine, passing the picture back to Middlebrook.

"Yes; it had a profound effect on her too," replied Middlebrook, anticipating the next question. He continued, "Initially she refused to watch it but I eventually brought her round with the promise that I would switch the video off the moment she felt uncomfortable with it. Eventually Alice watched the whole thing and I have to say it was a cathartic experience for her. This past week her attitude has improved dramatically."

"Zel-Enni referred to her as a prophet," stated Gerrard.

"Well she is in a way, Alice saw visions like no other person on the planet, as far as we know, and if she had had the presence of mind to stay calm and observe, maybe she could have warned us. But then like all prophets, who would have listened? She may still have ended up here. A thousand years ago she would have probably been burned as a witch."

The rest of the room concurred; there was no arguing this point.

"He talks of war but surely we could pursue a diplomatic solution first," enquired Wakefield.

Middlebrook shook his head. "This is an advanced race we are talking about. You just have to look back in history to see what advanced races have done. Take the Native Americans or the Aborigines, for example. All that diplomacy did for them was to incite genocide and the systematic destruction of a culture." He continued,

"Take the Egyptians as another example, do we care that we desecrate their graves when we excavated the pyramids?"

"But that was three – four thousand years ago for goodness sake," declared Ballentine.

"Exactly," replied Middlebrook excitedly, "these people are nearly half a million years ahead of us. We are like cavemen to them. We have what they want and they have nothing to lose." He paused with a sigh, "And there is no one more dangerous than that."

"Where are you getting this information?" enquired Ballentine with suspicion, "that wasn't mentioned on the video."

"I know," replied Middlebrook leaning back on his chair and pausing for a moment. "As I'm sure you'll remember I was late this morning. Well it actually was not my fault. I'd just got everything ready and was about leave my office with time to spare, when the most extraordinary thing happened…"

* * *

The meeting was scheduled for 11.30am and Middlebrook mentally congratulated himself on being ready to leave his office ten minutes early. Even he had to admit that generally his time keeping left a lot to be desired. He had arranged the documents into three piles on his desk and was about to pick them up when suddenly he heard a low drone that seemed to emanate from nowhere. He looked up and around trying to pin point the source of the sound. Then on the other side of his desk, about ten feet away, a bright yellow light appeared about six feet in the air. Small at first, then it started to grow, making a crackling sound. Middlebrook stood there transfixed by the apparition which began to slowly shoot out a yellow crackling light vertically downwards. When the light touched the floor there was an enormous flash and a loud crash of thunder. A blast of air hit Middlebrook full on and sent him crashing against the back wall. All the paperwork on his desk went flying into the air and dropped in chaos around the room. The desk shifted backwards also and Middlebrook slid down the wall slightly dazed. He looked up and could just about discern a black figure shrouded in a yellowy mist.

As the mist dissolved away the black figure became clear. At first he thought it was a robot but as the figure stood there motionless, Middlebrook heard a loud steady breathing emanating from what was obviously some sort of bio suit. The head had three blacked out slits for a visor and beneath that a hose fed down the chest and around the rear to a backpack. Either side were two circular vents, one facing forwards and one facing to the side and downwards. To Middlebrook it resembled a gas mask. At waist level there was a device fitted with a rectangular panel angled up to the wearer. This gave off a faint green glow against the suit, and either side were two vertical handles gripped tightly by gloved hands.

Middlebrook, gathering his senses, scrambled to his feet, spellbound by the sight. He stared with apprehension as the gloved hands moved to the neck of the suit and started fiddling with a clasp. A seal was broken with a hiss of air and with a slight twist the helmet was lifted off still attached to the hose. He braced himself in anticipation of seeing one of the creatures but what stood before him was a woman – a perfectly normal woman. Her hair was jet black and short, framing a reasonably attractive face that might have been prettier if it hadn't looked so drawn. She was about five feet six inches tall, in her early thirties but looked older.

"You're human!" exclaimed Middlebrook in astonishment.

"Yes," replied Earth's first time traveller nonchalantly, "but then so are the Devi's – well kind of."

"Devi's?" queried Middlebrook, gathering his wits together.

"Deviants, they hate being called that. They prefer Superior Homine."

"Err – higher than man," mused Middlebrook, trying to remember his Latin, "and are they?"

"In some ways yes, their IQ is off the charts but they are insane – brilliant but insane."

She stepped forward and extended her right arm in greeting. "Good morning Dr Middlebrook. My name is Karen." She smiled. "Karen Foster."

He shook her hand and replied, "The video implied that humans no longer exist in your time. Forgive my reaction."

"I know, Ds Zel-Enni was one of the better Devi's but even he had his limitations. He was economical with the truth. The Devi's developed a powerful drug which suppresses their psychoses and it works, up to a point. It does unfortunately have serious side effects. Apart from being highly addictive, it eventually fries their brains leaving them like vegetables. Zel used the drug sparingly with some success. The others mostly tend not to."

"You talk about him in the past tense,"

"He's dead! – executed for sending that message."

"That's a bit extreme isn't it?" said Middlebrook horrified.

"Well I did say they were mad."

"Why have they sent a human rather than a ... err Devi?" enquired Middlebrook.

"This is the first attempt to send somethi ... someone living," said Karen correcting herself. It was bad enough being dehumanised by the Devi's, she certainly wasn't going to contribute to it.

"My God!" said Middlebrook. "They're using you as a guinea pig."

Her face showed mild confusion since she didn't know what a guinea pig was. Karen decided to ignore the comment as her time was limited. She continued, "Look, I have been sent here to retrieve the message before you take it to the meeting, but don't worry I have no intention of taking it."

"What will you tell them?" said Middlebrook concerned for her.

"Don't worry – I will think of something."

"Why are they coming?"

"Our world is dying," said Karen with a sigh. Then she continued, "We don't know what happened but thousands and thousands of years ago we were forced underground by conditions on the surface. Those of us that went underground stayed as we are but those left on the surface evolved into the Deviants. Eventually our resources ran out and we were forced to the surface. Outnumbered by the Deviants we were captured and forced into a life of subjugation. And it's been that way now for centuries. They treat us like animals, though they allow someone like myself with higher intelligence to contribute, though in a limited capacity, like on this time machine project."

"What have we got that they could possibly want?" enquired Middlebrook, "our natural resources are depleted. They should have picked an earlier period in time."

"They have no choice over which time period to choose, for some reason we can only access this year. Maybe that will change as the technology improves. Who knows," said Karen with a shrug. Then she continued, "They are not interested in your fossil fuels, we have much cleaner power sources. No one knows for sure what they are up to. I'm afraid that I am not privy to that information. Some of my people have speculated that it might be for your water."

"My God," said Middlebrook again, astounded, "well, we certainly have plenty of that."

"That's an understatement!" exclaimed Karen. "Don't you realise that compared to us you are living in paradise. Our planet is eighty per cent desert. No seas. No rivers – and nearly all species of animals are extinct. What water we do retrieve is from deep underground and even that is running out."

"What the hell happened?" retorted Middlebrook.

"We don't know. We have nothing. No records at all beyond the last thirty thousand years. The legend that has been passed down through the centuries is that a powerful wind blew across the earth and behind it came the desert."

"All I can say for sure," she continued, "is that they are preparing for something massive."

Middlebrook observed the sadness in her eyes and realised her emaciated appearance was almost certainly due to too much work and not enough nourishment.

Karen suddenly felt dizzy and stumbled against the table.

"Are you alright?" enquired a concerned Middlebrook.

"It's your atmosphere, it's much richer in oxygen than ours."

"Have they stopped to think that changes to the past will make irrevocable changes to the future?" asked Middlebrook reasonably.

"You should see our future, maybe that would be a good thing," replied Karen. "In truth," she continued, "I don't think they know and frankly I don't think they even care. That's not all: they are also coming for Alice!" she warned. "The Devi's are fascinated by her and they want her baby. They will treat her like a lab rat, you must get her away – hide her."

"That's impossible. They're too late, Alice miscarried weeks ago."

Karen just shrugged; she had nothing else to add.

"Rats aren't extinct then," said Middlebrook; a hint of sarcasm in his voice.

"There will always be rats, don't you think?"

Middlebrook nodded sullenly, it seemed highly probable to him.

"Listen," urged Karen, "it is imperative that you make them listen at the meeting. Make it clear to them, the Deviants are coming and there is nothing that you can do to stop them. Prepare as best as you can."

A red light started flashing on her control panel. Startled, Karen looked at it and said, "This machine is programmed for a limited time and this light is a warning that I will return in sixty seconds." She started to get the helmet ready. Before she placed it on her head however, she opened a pocket on the right hand side of the suit and removed three objects.

"Take these," she said with urgency, "the two golden ones are for the meeting. They are further proof for those cynics that this is real. The blue one is for you personally. Keep it secret and act on it as soon as you can."

"One last thing," said Middlebrook. "Why have I been chosen to receive all this information?"

Karen smiled and said, "Because you are the only one who believed Alice."

As she pulled the helmet over her head Karen said, "Goodbye Dr Middlebrook, I doubt if we will ever meet again."

Just as she sealed the helmet to her suit there was a flash; not so loud this time and less violent, then she was gone. All that remained of her presence was a circular burn mark on the carpet about four feet in diameter.

Middlebrook stared still dazed by what had just transpired. Then he shook himself out of it and looked at his watch. He was ten minutes late already and he still needed to pick up the folders that had been scattered around the room.

Eventually he was ready to leave. He took the small blue envelope and locked it in his drawer. Then he took the two golden envelopes and put them in his inside jacket pocket. Sweeping up everything else from his desk, he dashed into the corridor and headed for the stairs.

* * *

"Well I've heard some excuses for being late in my time but that one takes the biscuit!" said Dr Rathburn, trying to inject a little humour in an attempt to break the silence that had descended on the room.

"I'm surprised no one heard the noise when she arrived," said Middlebrook.

The others looked at each other and shook their heads. The noise had gone unnoticed.

"So they are going to fight us over water," said Wakefield.

"Over the time we live in would be more accurate," replied Middlebrook.

"That would be intolerable," stated Wakefield, "we must resist them at all costs."

"Agreed," said Middlebrook, "though I would like to know how. Clearly their technology is way ahead of ours."

"We are not completely defenceless," said Ballentine.

"Get real for goodness sake," replied Middlebrook, forgetting himself, "they've got a bloody time machine. The mind boggles at what else they might have."

With the room falling silent and no one with anything to add, Middlebrook sensed that the meeting was drawing to a conclusion, so reaching into his inside jacket pocket he produced the two golden envelopes.

"What have you got there?" enquired Ballentine.

"I don't know, Karen gave me these two envelopes before she departed." He looked at Dr Rathburn but wouldn't make eye contact – she frowned, instinctively sensing that he was hiding something.

"I don't even know who they are for," stated Middlebrook. "I suppose the only way to find out is to open them."

He took one of the envelopes, broke the seal and lifted the flap. Inside was a gossamer light material: thin and translucent but very strong. Middlebrook took the material and unfolded it on the table. The sheet covered a good proportion of the table and appeared to be plans for something.

Ballentine leaned over for a closer look. "It looks to me like some kind of weapon but ..." he paused to look closer, "I don't recognise a lot of these symbols."

"Maybe you could take it and pass it to the right people," said Middlebrook, folding the sheet back up and passing it to Ballentine.

Ballentine nodded and put the plans back into the envelope. Middlebrook turned his attention to the second envelope and opened it.

Inside was a similar gossamer material which was much smaller when unfolded on the table. As he laid it down he saw a heading at the top.

"Oh Lord!" he exclaimed, "it's a cure for cancer."

"Let me see," said Gerrard pulling the sheet closer to him. He scanned his eyes over the information. "I haven't seen anything like it! – It says here it's a cure for all cancers."

"Well you seem to be best placed to do something with that," said Middlebrook sliding the sheet over to Gerrard. He then picked up the box which held the storage device, placed the DNA swab on top and passed it to Wakefield saying, "I think that you had better take this, the Prime Minister will need to see it."

Wakefield nodded gratefully; he thought that he would have had to confiscate the box for security reasons but Middlebrook surrendering it voluntarily saved any awkwardness.

The three ministers seemed more contrite now. The arrogance with which they had come into the meeting had completely gone. Middlebrook hoped that he had done enough to convince them.

"Well gentlemen," said Middlebrook bringing the meeting to a close, "now you know as much as I do. I hope you use this information wisely, I think we have difficult times ahead of us."

"What's your next step?" enquired Ballentine.

"Arrange for Alice's discharge from St. Clare's. She doesn't belong here." Middlebrook shook their hands, nodded to Dr Rathburn and left the room.

Dr Rathburn thanked the ministers for their patience as they stood up to leave. They shook her hand and one by one filtered out of the door. Now alone in the boardroom Dr Rathburn stood up and turned round to look out of the window. The well-manicured hospital grounds were in full bloom, the sun was shining; it was hard to believe that they were on the brink of Armageddon.

Her thoughts turned to Middlebrook. What was he hiding? She was going to have to interrogate him.

* * *

It is the general consensus that in times of calamity, all nations of the world would put away their differences of race, colour and creed and unite against a common foe for the greater good of everyone. At least this is what Middlebrook hoped as he sat in his office contemplating the future. It was late Friday afternoon, about half an hour after he had left the boardroom. He had come back to an office in disarray. One side of his desk had shifted about two feet, his chair was on its side and the paperwork on his desk was strewn all over the floor. After a quick tidy up he sat back in his chair, put his feet up on the desk and placed his hands over his face. It had been an eventful and tiring day. He thought of the three ministers: they had entered the room as Three Wise Monkeys, and after taking away their three gifts, it occurred to him that they were leaving like the Three Wise Men. Middlebrook couldn't help but laugh at this thought, but it was no laughing matter really; their wisdom to follow through with the information given to them was imperative. *We may not have much defence but at least we would go down fighting*, he thought. Suddenly the door opened and Dr Rathburn entered the room.

Middlebrook, interrupted from his contemplation, took his feet off the desk and said, "Have they gone?"

"Yes," nodded Dr Rathburn.

"Did they say anything before they left?"

"Not much, I think you've given them plenty to ponder over."

Middlebrook nodded and said nothing, this being an understatement.

Dr Rathburn leant back against the door and stared at Middlebrook. Eventually he could stand it no longer and with his arms stretched out towards her simply said, "What?"

"Come on Barny, this is me you are talking to. I know you. What were you holding back at the meeting when you handed out those envelopes?"

Middlebrook stared back and eventually sighed in defeat. It was true; he could never keep anything from her. Fishing out a key from his trouser pocket, he unlocked the drawer and removed the blue envelope given to him by Karen.

"She told me to keep it a secret," said Middlebrook as he started to open the envelope.

"You got one too," said Dr Rathburn, her interest piqued.

Inside was a slip of paper with a series of numbers on it. Middlebrook studied them for a minute then turned the envelope towards Dr Rathburn and said, "Any ideas?"

"No," frowned Dr Rathburn after examining the numbers, "they just look completely random to me."

Taking a black marker pen from his desk, Middlebrook wrote the numbers down on a white board fixed to his wall. Then both of them stood there studying the sequence of numbers. A knock at the door jolted them from their deliberation.

"Come in," said Middlebrook still staring at the board.

It was Mrs Davies, the cleaning lady. She was a middle-aged woman wearing beige slacks and a pink tabard.

"Can I clean your office Dr Middlebrook?" she said sheepishly, after noticing Dr Rathburn in the room as well.

"Err – yes – of course," replied Middlebrook, trying not to be distracted.

Mrs Davies busied herself dusting but couldn't help but look at what they were staring at. Finally she said, "Choosing your lottery numbers are you?"

"What?" replied Middlebrook, forgetting his manners.

"Lottery numbers!" exclaimed Mrs. Davies.

They both looked at the board then looked at each other in realisation.

"Lottery numbers!" they shouted in unison. Neither of them had ever done the lottery so consequently didn't understand their significance.

"She said act on them as soon as possible but the lottery isn't until tomorrow, isn't it?" said Middlebrook.

"Oh no dear," said Mrs Davies, "it's not the Saturday lottery. It's the European lottery tonight."

"How do you know?" enquired Dr Rathburn.

"Well," continued Mrs Davies, "there are seven numbers instead of six and these two are duplicated. See." She pointed at the second and sixth number in the sequence as if this would make it any clearer to them. It didn't. Mrs Davies looked at her watch and said, "You'd better hurry, it's six twenty: the draw for tonight closes soon."

Middlebrook dashed to his deck, picked up his car keys and the numbers then pulled Dr Rathburn towards the door.

Mrs Davies continued talking, "Good luck dears, it's a rollover of twenty one milli…" She didn't get to finish her sentence, Middlebrook and Dr Rathburn had gone.

Shaking her head in disbelief, Mrs Davies pulled her vacuum cleaner into the office and then frowned as she saw that the round burn mark on the carpet had become even bigger.

* * *

That evening around nine o'clock they were sitting on the sofa at Dr Anna Rathburn"s house, both staring at a pink slip of paper worth twenty-one million pounds.

"Oh my God!" exclaimed Anna in disbelief.

"Will you stop saying that," said Middlebrook, his mind racing.

"Sorry," replied Anna, "it's just … twenty-one million!"

"I know, I know," said Middlebrook trying to calm down and think rationally. He could see his objectives rapidly going down the drain.

"Look Anna," he continued, "I've made plans for this weekend and this has kind of put a spanner in the works."

"What plans?"

"I intend to take Alice out of St. Clare's tomorrow and take her up to Cumbria."

"Cumbria? Why there?"

"I inherited a holiday cottage from my folks in the village of Elter Water. I use it as a pied-a-terre. I thought that we could hide out there until we decide what to do next."

"Oh, right," replied Anna. She hadn't given much thought to the fact that he would be leaving. But it made sense in the circumstances.

Middlebrook observed her reaction, and then said, "Why don't you come with us?"

Anna was confused: on the one hand she was pleased to be asked but on the other she was annoyed that he had just dropped it in her lap, almost as an afterthought.

"I don't know Barny, there is so much to consider. My job, the house…"

"I understand," interrupted Middlebrook, a little disappointed.

"Does Alice know of your intentions?" asked Anna changing the subject quickly.

"No, at least this way she won't have time to dwell on leaving. I don't want to give her the opportunity to change her mind."

"I can't come straightaway," replied Anna getting back to the point, "someone needs to redeem this ticket."

"Yes – of course," said Middlebrook. He thought for a second. "Have you got a pen and paper handy?"

Anna got up, moved to a sideboard and returned with a notepad and pen. She passed them to Middlebrook who started writing.

"This is my address and phone number at the cottage," he said. "Phone me only if you have to, but not from your mobile."

"I understand,"

"I really must go now," said Middlebrook standing up, "I'm shattered and I've got a busy weekend ahead. Promise me you'll think about coming."

"Yes – I promise," she replied. Then said with a cheeky grin, "Are you sure you want to trust me with all this money?"

"You are the only person I do trust," he said, smiling back.

Finally Middlebrook gave Anna a peck on the cheek, she wished him good luck and then he left.

Anna closed the door, wondering whether she would ever see him again.

* * *

As Middlebrook drove up to the front of St. Clare's, it occurred to him what a dark and foreboding post-Victorian edifice it was. He had always looked forward to working, and indeed made his reputation here, but now it looked different to him. Or maybe he had changed. The fact that someone like Alice, who should never have been admitted in the first place could end up here upset him more than he was prepared to admit and made him question his judgement. At least he could do something to put things right.

Parking his car, Middlebrook made his way into the hospital, saying hello to the staff on reception then heading straight to Alice's dormitory. He stopped at the door and knocked.

"Who is it?" came a timid voice.

"It's me – Dr Middlebrook."

The door opened gingerly and there stood Alice still in her dressing gown. She had just had a shower and her hair was still wet.

"What are you doing here? – it's Saturday," Alice enquired not unreasonably since she hardly ever saw him at weekends.

Middlebrook sat on the end of the bed and patted the duvet for her to sit next to him. Alice sat down and looked at him expectantly. He could see that with reduced medication and the knowledge that her apparitions were real, Alice's appearance had greatly improved.

"I want you to pack your things," said Middlebrook, "I'm taking you out of here this morning."

"But I feel safe here," said Alice.

"You're not safe here anymore. The Deviants know that you are here, we need to get away."

"Where are we going?"

"The Lake District, I have a place there. We should be safe there for a while."

Alice glanced over her shoulder at some discarded clothes. "I don't want any of these things," she said, "they belong to the old me. I want to buy some new clothes. I have money."

It seemed reasonable to Middlebrook, if that's what it would take to help her move on.

"Okay then," he soothed, "we can go shopping today and travel up there tomorrow. But you'll have to put something on – I'm not taking you shopping naked," he joked. "Oh and don't worry about money, it's not a problem."

Alice chuckled and rested her head on his shoulder. "I'm frightened."

You and me both, thought Middlebrook, though he kept it to himself.

"Is Dr Rathburn coming?" asked Alice suddenly.

Middlebrook was taken aback by this question. Why would Alice ask such a thing?

"Err – I don't know," he replied, "she said that she would think about it."

"You should have told her how you feel about her," continued Alice.

Since Middlebrook was not entirely sure how he felt himself, he found this all a little bit unnerving.

"Where are you getting all this from?"

"I don't know – I just sense it," said Alice enigmatically.

Middlebrook decided not to pursue the subject any further, they needed to get going. He would broach the subject some other time. Alice was a constant source of amazement to him.

She got dressed while Middlebrook sorted out her discharge from the hospital and soon they were driving away from St. Clare's and heading for the shops.

* * *

Whilst Alice and Middlebrook were travelling up to Cumbria, Anna spent the weekend planning the following week. Firstly, she needed to cash the lottery ticket. She would make the phone call on Monday. Then there was the question of where to put it. The obvious answer to her was a numbered Swiss bank account but she had no idea how to open one. It also occurred to her that it might be a good idea to give a bequest to Alice's husband, John. Okay, so he hadn't acquitted himself very well but he had still been put through the mill and deserved something. Anna decided to appoint a solicitor to deal with the payment to John. At least that way it could be kept confidential. After some research on the Internet it became clear that Anna was going to have to make a trip to Geneva in Switzerland to open a Swiss bank account, so she dug out an overnight suitcase from her wardrobe and located her passport.

Late Sunday afternoon, Anna was making herself some dinner when there was a knock at the door. She opened the door to see two strange men standing there. Both were tall and slim wearing black Macintosh coats despite the fact that it was dry and warm. Their faces were fairly nondescript except for the fact that they were both bald and wearing dark sunglasses. If the sight was intended to intimidate then it was working.

"Can I help you?" said a hesitant Anna.

"Forgive the intrusion Dr Rathburn but we need to ask you some questions," said one of the men. The stranger had a monotone voice with a mild mid-Atlantic accent. Before Anna could respond they both pushed past her and made their way into the hall.

"Excuse me but you can't..." spluttered Anna.

"Oh but we can," said the same man interrupting her. Then he gestured to the living room and said, "Shall we?"

Anna walked past them nervously and they followed her in. She sat in an armchair; the two men sat on the sofa.

"We need to ask you some questions about Dr Barnabus Middlebrook and Alice Denham," said the second man.

Anna could see where this was going and needed to gather her wits about her. She decided to stall for time.

"Who are you?" she demanded. "Have you any ID?"

"I'm afraid our identity is a matter of national security," said the first man, "we have no ID."

"What do you want to know?" asked Anna.

"Dr Middlebrook discharged Mrs Denham from St. Clare's on Saturday and they haven't been seen since," said the second man, watching Anna closely to gauge her reaction.

"Gone?" replied Anna incredulously. "I don't understand," she continued, trying hard to sound convincing.

"You mean you have no idea where they are?" said the first man.

"No – of course not, this is all news to me."

"We must find them – for their own safety, you understand," said the second man. "Is there anywhere that you know of where he might have taken her?"

"I'm sorry, no," replied Anna, "we weren't that close." Anna surprised herself in being able to lie so easily, especially when put under pressure. She hoped that they believed her; she just wanted them out of her house.

The two men stared at her for an inordinately long time hoping that she might crack but Anna held her nerve. She instinctively knew not to volunteer anything that might prolong this – what could only be described as an informal interrogation. Eventually the first man stood up and the second followed.

"If you hear anything you can contact this number," said the first man placing a card into Anna's hand.

"Okay," said Anna simply, looking at the card. It was plain white with a phone number printed in black, and nothing else.

As they walked to the front door Anna asked, "Do I need a name?"

"No," came a curt reply. One of them opened the door and they were gone, walking down her driveway.

Anna closed the door and leant against it giving out a big sigh of relief.

Who were they? she thought. *Obviously someone is taking this seriously.*

Later that evening, Anna went upstairs to close her curtains and as she gazed out in the half light, she noticed a strange black 4x4 car parked across the road and a little way back. It may be nothing but she wrote down the licence plate number anyway.

In the morning, Anna woke up early and the first thing that she thought of was the strange black car. She slipped out of bed and moved to the side of the window. With the minimum of movement of the curtains she was able to see down the road. The car was still there. Obviously she was going to have to revise her plans. Instead of phoning the lottery she decided to go into work and act as normal – at least until she knew what this car was up to. Before she left her house she put her passport, the lottery ticket and Middlebrook's address in her handbag for safe keeping, then as she drove away from her house to go to St. Clare's later that morning, she noticed the black car following, a few cars behind. That decided it, she was going to have to bide her time.

By Thursday morning, Anna was starting to get really annoyed. She had been shadowed for three days now and it wasn't letting up.

The day dragged by and Anna was starting to get a little unnerved. Finding it difficult to concentrate, she decided to leave work early. When she got home however, she was horrified to see that her front door lock had been broken. Gingerly she opened the door and walked in. Straightaway it was clear that the house had been ransacked. Drawers were pulled out, their contents strewn all over the floor. The chairs in the living room were ripped open; it was the same all over the house.

Having a good idea who was responsible, Anna wasn't sure whether to call the police or not. It was a dilemma: calling the police would draw attention, but it would be the normal thing to do. That decided it, she must make the call. The police were there for ages asking questions and taking a statement, until eventually, after doing all that they could for the time being, left her to it. Anna didn't feel comfortable in a house that had just been burgled but she was too tired to care so after arranging for a locksmith and sorting out her bedroom as best as she could, Anna got ready for bed. Just before settling down for the night she went to the window to close the curtains and noticed that the strange black car was nowhere to be seen.

The black car was absent on Friday morning too, nor was it evident over the weekend, to the point that Anna started to relax a little by Sunday evening and began thinking about the plans that she had made the week before.

* * *

On the ninety minute flight to Geneva, Anna just had time to reflect on the previous two days. Monday was a day of making phone calls. Firstly, she arranged to cash the lottery ticket the next day, then she phoned a solicitor and arranged a meeting for Thursday afternoon to discuss John's bequest. Finally, she booked a flight to Switzerland and an overnight stay in a hotel. It was now Wednesday morning and she hoped that there wouldn't be any problems to delay her. She didn't want to have to reschedule the solicitor's meeting.

After a while her thoughts turned to Barny; she still hadn't decided whether to join him in Cumbria. She would be giving up an awful lot, especially her career.

On the other hand, if the near future for Earth is to be an apocalyptic war and the twenty-one million pound cheque in her handbag was tangible proof of that fact, then would she have a career anyway.

Anna had always hoped that something romantic might have happened between them but she had to admit they were as bad as each other, being too career minded – too wrapped up in their own work.

Soon the plane landed and she was heading for passport control. As she approached Anna dipped into her handbag and pulled out her passport. Along with it came the address that Middlebrook had given her. She stared at it for a minute then screwed it up in her hand and threw it in a litter bin. Anna had made up her mind; she knew exactly what she was going to do.

CHAPTER FOUR
GO WEST YOUNG WOMAN

Dr Barnabus Middlebrook sat on a large boulder overlooking Elter Water Lake. For the past fortnight it had become his favourite spot at this time of day, a place where he could think things through. It was late afternoon and he could enjoy the splendour of the Langdale Pikes rising up some distance away on the other side of the lake. Now they were partially obscured by an autumnal mist which had started to bubble up, and was slowly, but steadily, heading his way. It had been an overcast day and the shadowy nature of the light gave the water an inky-black quality; bestowing the whole vista with a very eerie atmosphere. In the present circumstances, the portentous aspect of the scene was not lost on him.

The sound of footsteps on the path behind shook him from his reverie and he looked round expecting to see Alice walking towards him. What he saw however, was Dr Anna Rathburn heading his way. She was dressed casually in faded jeans, trainers and a light blue hooded sweatshirt. Her hair was down just below her shoulders, her make-up was much lighter than usual and as Middlebrook watched her approach she smiled in greeting. It occurred to Middlebrook: why on earth it had taken him so long to notice how pretty she was.

He smiled back and said, "Hi – at last you've got here. Pull up a rock and make yourself comfortable."

Anna chuckled and sat down on the boulder next to him.

"It's been a horrendous two weeks, I'll tell you about it later."

"You look good," he said relieved that she had finally arrived. Middlebrook wasn't at all certain that she would.

"Well thank you kind sir," replied Anna surprised at the compliment, especially from him.

"You don't look so bad yourself," she continued, "funny how you seem to look smarter when you dress down."

They laughed and then both looked across the lake noticing the mist getting ever closer.

"I dropped my things off at the cottage," said Anna. "It's gorgeous. I could stay here forever."

"Did you see Alice?" enquired Middlebrook, ignoring the comment.

"Yes, she was in the kitchen cooking dinner. What a difference these two weeks have made to her. She's looking so much better."

Middlebrook nodded. "She's eating and sleeping normally and she goes out every morning for a run, often up to five miles, and spends a lot of her time exercising in the cottage. Physically she is getting very fit,"

"And mentally?" asked Anna with trepidation.

"She's not a hundred percent, but she's getting there."

"I don't think any of us are a hundred percent," observed Anna.

"Speak for yourself," joked Middlebrook.

Anna nudged him and he slid off the boulder and landed on his feet. Middlebrook turned to her and said,

"It would be nice if we could pass some money on to John."

"I've already dealt with it," said Anna, "at least his financial worries are over." Then she continued, "Does Alice talk about him at all?"

"She did, a little at first," replied Middlebrook, solemnly climbing back onto the boulder, "but not at all now. I think she feels badly let down by him; the way she sees it, if John hadn't put that mirror back on the bathroom wall she might not have lost her baby."

"Well I must admit she does have a point there," observed Anna, "is she talking at all about her experiences at the house?"

"Yes, though she has sublimated her fear with anger and resentment. As far as she is concerned those Deviants destroyed her family – her whole world! I think she is looking for revenge. If nothing else, at least she has her spirit back," he continued, "she has also started displaying cognitive abilities and might even be precognitive too."

Anna nodded sombrely and they sat in silence for a while as the mist started to creep up the side of the shore.

"Thanks for coming," said Middlebrook finally, and with feeling.

"Thank you for asking me," replied Anna, with a shiver.

The mist had started to roll over them and the temperature had started to drop. Middlebrook took the opportunity to put his arm around her and pulled her towards him. Anna turned her head towards his and they kissed gently on the lips. She put her arms around him and they kissed again, this time more passionately.

"That took you long enough," she said with a smile.

"I was waiting for the right moment," replied Middlebrook pathetically.

"Yes but ten years!" admonished Anna jokingly.

They sat arm in arm on the boulder until eventually Anna asked, "What's our next step?"

"We need somewhere, where we can disappear," mused Middlebrook. "I'm damned if I am going to let those things take Alice. I was thinking maybe Australia or perhaps Europe,"

"No! We need somewhere more practical," said Anna assertively, "America – we can disappear there."

Middlebrook nodded in agreement, surprised that he didn't think of the USA himself. Sliding off the boulder Middlebrook helped Anna down.

"We'd better get back," he said, "it's starting to get dark."

As they began to make their way back to the cottage a figure emerged from the mist which had swept past them. It was Alice wearing grey camouflaged combat trousers and a grey strappy top. This showed off her broader shoulders and developing arm muscles. Her hair was cut short in a boyish fashion and dyed blonde, the whole impression was of a completely different woman.

"Hey you two!" she called cheerfully, "dinner's ready."

They both smiled, glad to see Alice so upbeat.

"Alice," hailed Middlebrook – how do you fancy America?"

"Sounds good," said Alice matter-of-factly. "America will work. We can buy weapons in America."

Anna and Middlebrook looked at each other, a little startled at her reply. Alice just smiled back, and said nothing more. She had an agenda all of her own.

Anna turned and looked at Alice and as they made eye contact, Alice felt a rushing sensation in her mind which got faster and faster. Alice, in her mind, seemingly transformed to a different place, was there but not there at the same time. Her surroundings were completely different. Standing in an unfamiliar environment Alice was able to observe Anna sitting in a chair in what looked like a large wooden hut. Anna was holding two babies in her arms, one of which was normal, while the other had abnormally large eyes. Shining bright blue. There were other people present, none of whom Alice recognised and Middlebrook was to one side looking down at Anna.

They both looked at Alice curiously, who appeared to be in a trance like state; transfixed to the spot. Suddenly the vision disappeared and Alice was jolted back to reality.

"Are you alright?" asked Anna, who had noticed a sudden change in her.

"Um – yes I'm fine," answered Alice who was inwardly shaken by the experience. Neither were convinced by her reply but decided not to pursue it any further for the time being.

Middlebrook and Anna caught up with Alice and together they made their way towards the cottage, the thick mist was swirling around them now, making the way ahead demanding and unclear.

PART TWO

NOR HELL A FURY

CHAPTER FIVE
URSUS ARCTOS HORRIBILIS

Joseph Borowski picked up his Colt AR15 semi-automatic rifle, pulled back the bolt handle, loaded a bullet into the breach and switched the gun to safety. Then he picked up his cap, placed it firmly on his head and stepped out of the tent that was currently being used by the troops to bunk down in. Joe looked around him taking in the clearing and the tree line beyond, in the distance the Cabinet Mountain range loomed majestically with its snow covered peaks.

A matt olive green Humvee with a gun emplacement on the roof screeched to a halt nearby spraying muddy water from the previous night's rain. The gunner looked down at Joe apologetically and slid down into the cabin. Distracted from the view, his attention was drawn to the activity in the camp. Tents surrounded the clearing and both men and women dressed in battle fatigues were running around all seemingly with some task in mind though it seemed like organised chaos to Joe.

A man suddenly came into view from behind the Humvee. He was also dressed in fatigues though they didn't quite sit so well on him. Joe smiled in recognition – it was Barnabus Middlebrook, who, as he approached, was smiling back tentatively.

"Doc, how are ya?" hailed Joe, trying to stay upbeat. He knew why Middlebrook was coming over.

"Hello Joe, did you manage to speak to Alice last night?"

"Sure I did." Joe shook his head resignedly, "It made no difference though, she is determined to go today and that's it."

Middlebrook looked despondent: both he and Anna had tried to convince Alice that going on this sortie was foolhardy to say the least but she wouldn't listen, so they hoped that Joe would be able to talk some sense into her.

"Look Doc, I'm with you on this but you know what she's like. Alice is her own woman and she is determined to go out there and kick some ass and frankly woe betide anyone who gets in her way."

"I know," replied Middlebrook, "at least you tried. Keep an eye on her won't you and look after yourself?"

Joe nodded, shook Middlebrook's hand and watched him walk across the clearing back to the RV.

"Has he gone?"

Joe's head whipped round to the right to see Alice close behind him. Slightly startled Joe said, "Where did you spring from?"

"I saw Barny talking to you so I decided to stand back until he left."

"Are you trying to avoid him?"

"You could say that, I'm not in the mood for another lecture, that's all."

Alice walked round and stood in front of him looking every bit the army grunt. Joe looked her up and down; she was wearing full battle dress of flak jacket and camouflaged trousers tucked into black leather boots.

Over her right shoulder she carried a Colt AR15 rifle and as she pulled her cap onto her head, she said, "Come on we're late, it's time for the briefing."

Joe nodded, fell in beside her and as they both walked across the clearing a light shower began to fall.

* * *

A crowd of troops had gathered in the middle of the clearing by the time they got there, Alice and Joe mingled with them. Everyone was looking at the back of an army truck from where they expected General Glenn Jackson to emerge. Alice moved to the front to get a better view but Joe stayed at the back happy where he was.

"She's going to get us all killed, you know that don't you."

Joe looked round to see Katlin Grody standing beside him looking to the front like everyone else.

"None of this is her fault I know that," said Joe somewhat irritably.

"Yeah but she's reckless and has no regard for her own safety. It makes her a danger to others," Katlin was now looking up at Joe in a more pleading manner.

"You've never liked her, right from the beginning."

"She didn't give me much option," replied Katlin who stormed off into the throng of troops.

Before Joe could dwell on her words General Jackson appeared from the back of the truck. Cheers and hollers went up from the crowd but he smiled and raised his right arm to quell the greeting. He looked around at the ninety plus men and a few women who were looking up at him with expectant faces. Finally, he spoke.

"People, as you are aware the Deviants, or Black Eyes as I prefer to call them, have the whole planet secured and placed under their own martial law. It's only pockets of resistance like us that can take the fight back to them. We have weapons and ammunition but we need more if we are to continue to be effective in any way. Before I made my escape, I was able to bring with me a number of maps."

General Jackson stepped to one side to reveal a map hanging from the back of the truck. He picked up a baton and pointed to an area on the map.

"This map covers the states of Washington, Oregon, Idaho, Montana and Wyoming. On it are marked two locations – underground bases where caches of weapons have been stored." He looked back at the troops and smiled. "The government has always denied the existence of these bases but I can confirm to you now that they do in fact exist. It's not often that our politicians get things right."

Subdued laughter rose up from the crowd and quickly subsided.

"There is one of these caches about ninety miles south of here." General Jackson pointed to it on the map. "But there is a problem. Close by is a Black Eye outpost and our activity may well alert it."

Jackson paused and gave the crowd a steely stare and then said, "This is a dangerous mission people but if we are to continue the fight we must have those weapons. Are you with me?"

The crowd cheered then Jackson shouted again, "are you with me?"

The troops roared their approval. Satisfied Jackson said finally, "That only leaves me to wish you luck and hand you over to your company commander who will brief you in more detail." Jackson turned and disappeared into the back of the truck and the crowd started to disperse.

Alice came bounding up to Joe excited and said, "Some action at last Joe."

"Be careful what you wish for Alice," he said less enthusiastically and then to himself he thought: *be careful what you wish for*.

* * *

The convoy of trucks moved south out of the camp heading towards their rendezvous. In the back of the third truck sat Joe, opposite him sat Alice. To her left was Emilio Cardenas, a loud mouthed Mexican, and next to him was Katlin. Sitting next to Joe was an African American called Sherman; a giant of a man who said very little. The remainder of the troops in the truck were less familiar to Joe.

After a while, Joe became aware of the fact that Cardenas was staring at him. Then Cardenas turned to Alice and said, "Hey limey – you ever considered seeing someone with balls?"

Alice looked at him dispassionately and replied, "sorry but I'm not interested in men whose parents are related."

Joe and Katlin began to chuckle.

"What so funny?" asked a confused Cardenas.

"She's calling you a retard you jackass," laughed Katlin.

By now everyone was laughing and a humiliated Cardenas said, "Well fuck you Grody."

"Yeah, well fuck you too," retorted Katlin, not in the least bit intimidated.

Seeing the banter getting out of hand Joe interjected, "Okay. Okay pipe down everyone. Let's save it for the enemy, eh?"

Emilio Cardenas, having grown up in the slums of Mexico City, was a tough son-of-a-bitch who didn't back down from anybody. He may not have been the sharpest tool in the box but he was reliable under fire and would always have your back when needed. Never knowing when to shut up though, he turned his attention to the large black man sitting opposite him.

"Hey Sherman, is that your real name?" bellowed Cardenas.

"Of course it's not his real name," interrupted Katlin who could be equally loquacious when the mood took her, "he's named after the tank because of his size."

"Is that right?" enquired Cardenas.

"Maybe," Sherman replied laconically.

"Mind you it could be because of the size of his weapon," laughed Katlin lasciviously.

"Yeah," said Sherman dimwittedly, missing the innuendo and picking up his over-sized gun by the barrel.

"Jesus!" exclaimed Cardenas, "that's a 50 calibre M2."

"Yeah," said Sherman again, "I rescued it from a busted up hummer."

Cardenas shook his head in disbelief and finally fell silent. Joe, still smiling to himself, caught Alice smiling back at him and his thoughts went back to the day when they first met only two weeks ago …

* * *

Alice finally stopped jogging and slipped her back pack and rifle from off of her shoulders. Still panting from the run up the steady incline of the Cabinet Mountain Range, she sat down on a fallen tree and looked over the scenery. The Kaniksu National Forest looked particularly beautiful in late spring with beams of sunlight streaming through the branches of the fir, pine and spruce, pointing silently at the sky. As Alice turned her head she could make out the Selkirk mountain range looming in the distance. All this was a far cry from the UK which she, Anna and Middlebrook had left behind six months earlier. Despite being mid-May there was still a nip in the air, though Alice barely noticed it after her arduous climb up the slope.

After a while, she opened her rucksack and pulled out a drinks bottle and emptied half of it in one guzzle. Then she grabbed a target and some pins. Alice walked over to a tree about fifty feet away and fixed the target to it. Walking back to a fallen tree, she picked up her rifle, stepped over the trunk and lay on the ground just behind it. Using the trunk as a rest, Alice took aim at the target. Her first shot clipped the side of the trunk so she got herself more comfortable and tried again. This time she could see that she was on target. Several shots later, Alice walked down to the target and checked her results. She had been practising now for two weeks and was a little dismayed to see her grouping was still erratic. With a new target fixed to the tree she walked back to the trunk, settled behind it to try again. There was little improvement on her second attempt – Alice frowned and pulled the target off the tree. Then she looked at her watch, it was mid-afternoon so decided it was time to make her way back, but not before one last look at the magnificent view of the Selkirk mountain range. Walking back to her rucksack she picked it up and loaded it onto her shoulder then picked up her rifle.

As she started to move up the slope to get a better view, a fearsome roar came from out of the bushes to her right. Startled, Alice side stepped and slid into a small depression and got her left foot jammed under an exposed tree root. Pain shot up her leg and she gave out a muted squeal. Again there came an angry growl and Alice could see a grizzly bear bearing down on her from out of the bushes. Panicking she tried to scramble for her rifle which was just out of reach. The bear now on its hind legs looked huge looming over Alice who was desperately trying to grab the gun. Just as she got hold of the end of the barrel Alice heard a loud shot. The bear stopped in its tracks then there was another loud shot, and the bear turned tail and disappeared into the bush. A man with a shotgun looked down at Alice then went to check on the grizzly which was scuttling away with two cubs following close behind. The bear gave one last look back and then silently disappeared into the trees. Satisfied the threat was over he turned his attention to the girl sitting below him with her foot firmly wedged under a tree root.

"Are you okay?" said the stranger walking down to Alice.

"Do I look okay?" replied winced Alice, annoyed to be found in such a vulnerable situation.

The man smiled and bent down at Alice's foot to get a closer look. He was about six feet tall, slim but well built. His hair was short and dark with a hint of grey at the sides. Alice guessed him to be in his early to mid-thirties.

"It's lucky for you I turned up."

"I had it under control," replied an indignant Alice, "I'd already grabbed hold of my rifle."

The man picked up Alice's gun; it was a CZ 452 Ultra target rifle.

"This pee shooter," he laughed, "it would only have pissed her off more."

"How do you know it was a she?" enquired Alice.

"She had two cubs in tow. That's a why she was showing aggression – you probably startled her."

"I startled her," replied an incredulous Alice, then after considering it for a few seconds said, "I didn't know about the cubs. Were they cute?"

The man smiled, held out his right hand and said, "My name is Joe Borowski."

Alice shook his hand and replied, "Alice – Alice Denham. Now are you going to get my foot out of this root or not."

"Okay, okay," laughed Joe, "jeez you're more ornery than the bear."

"Look could you please get it out – it hurts." Alice grimaced.

With as much care as possible Joe manoeuvred Alice's foot free while she winced at the pain.

"Can you move your ankle?" enquired Joe.

Alice gingerly started to rotate her ankle trying not to show too much discomfort.

"Well I don't think it's broken."

"How do you know, are you a doctor?"

"I'm an animal doctor," stated Joe.

"A vet then – that makes you perfectly qualified," replied a sarcastic Alice.

"You're an animal aren't you? And besides it's the best you are gonna get up here right now. Let's see if you can stand on it."

Joe helped Alice to her feet and she tried to put her weight on it. Immediately she squealed and Joe had to support her. "Looks like I'm taking you home."

He paused and then said, "Where does a Brit stuck in the middle of the Idaho panhandle live anyway?"

"I'm not a Brit as you so eloquently put it, I'm English," said Alice getting slightly indignant again.

"What's the difference?" enquired Joe.

"God, where do I start," replied Alice half to herself, "we're camped about five miles that way."

Alice pointed down the hill in the direction she had come.

"There are more of you then?" said Joe.

"I'm travelling with two others in a large RV."

"What were you doing up here?" enquired Joe.

"Enjoying your wonderful scenery and getting some target practice in," said Alice succinctly.

"Right," said Joe, not knowing how seriously to take her.

With Alice leaning on Joe for support they made their way slowly down the hill. It was starting to get dark when they finally arrived at the clearing where the RV was parked.

* * *

"It's getting late," said a concerned looking Anna glancing at her watch, "the sun is going down behind the trees."

"I know," replied Middlebrook echoing her concern.

If this went on much longer he was going to have to go out looking for her. Both looked anxiously at the tree line as the light was starting to fade. They were sat at a patio table drinking coffee and just as Middlebrook got up realising that he was going to have to go looking before it got too dark, two figures came hobbling out of the trees.

"Alice," shouted Anna seeing her first.

Middlebrook looked round and saw them also. Alice had clearly hurt herself and was being supported by some stranger. Immediately, he rushed over to help with Anna following close behind.

"My God, are you alright?" said Middlebrook showing his anguish but feeling relief that she was back in one piece.

"You had us worried sick," added Anna, "what happened?"

"Can I just get to a chair," winced Alice, "I really need to sit down."

Helping her over to the table and chairs, they sat an exhausted Alice down. As she looked up, Alice noticed Anna and Middlebrook's attention had turned to the man standing opposite them.

"This is Joe – he saved my life," said Alice matter-of-factly.

Joe held out his hand with a faint smile.

"Barnabus Middlebrook, and this is Anna Rathburn," said Middlebrook smiling back.

They both shook hands with Joe and invited him to sit down.

"Would you like some coffee," enquired Anna still smiling at Joe.

"That would be great ma'am," replied Joe, wondering what English coffee might taste like.

Anna stepped up into the RV and quickly returned carrying a tray with coffee and extra cups.

"Black, no sugar," said Joe anticipating her next question. Anna duly poured him a cup and then went round the table filling everyone else's. Joe took a tentative sip, surprised to find that it was actually very good. He took a larger gulp and enjoyed the warmth as the hot liquid flowed down into his stomach.

"So," said Middlebrook finally, "what happened out there?"

Alice and Joe between them imparted the whole incident whilst Anna and Middlebrook listened in silence raising their eyebrows in alarm when the bear was mentioned.

"I tried to tell her that the woods were dangerous, but would she listen?" said Anna rhetorically.

"If I stayed around here all day I'd go stir crazy," replied Alice petulantly.

Joe smiled then looked at these three Brits, who to him looked completely out of place in this wilderness. It was clear that Anna and Middlebrook were much older than Alice and were possibly an item, so what was the relationship with Alice. She was clearly too old to be their daughter.

"Joe would you like something to eat?" asked Anna, "you must both be starving."

"Not for me thanks," yawned Joe looking at his watch, "it's getting late and I should really be getting back." Then Joe looked at Middlebrook and said, "Would it be possible to get a ride out to my pick-up? It's about an hour's drive from here."

"Of course," said Middlebrook, "it's the least we can do. I'll just put Alice's rifle away and we can get going."

Joe watched as Middlebrook unlocked the luggage compartment in the side of the RV and placed the rifle inside. It was dark now but he was pretty sure that he had noticed other weapons in the compartment.

As Middlebrook returned, Joe looked at Alice who had managed to get to her feet. She limped towards him and said, "I didn't thank you for saving my life."

"That's okay – all in a day's work," smiled Joe modestly.

Alice leant forwards and gave him a kiss on the cheek. Then suddenly she felt her mind racing again, rushing forwards at great speed. Her stare was fixed on Joe but she seemed to be looking straight through him. In her mind Alice was in a beautiful alcove by the sea. Rocks wrapped around the beach to give it a large measure of seclusion. The sea was gently lapping up the beach and the sun was pleasantly warm. Like before Alice felt as though she was there but not there at the same time. Scanning the alcove, Alice's attention came upon a figure starting to stand up. The figure was emanating a bright light and Alice had to shield her eyes. As they adjusted, Alice could just make out who the figure was. It was Joe and behind him stood a shadowy figure, obscured by the bright light. Joe was standing now and starting to walk towards her smiling. At this moment the mysterious shadowy figure suddenly vanished and Alice came back to her senses with a jolt. The whole experience only lasted about five seconds but it didn't go unnoticed with Anna who had seen it once before.

"Are you okay?" said Joe.

Alice smiled and nodded, "I'm fine," she lied, "just tired that's all."

"It was nice to have met you Joe," interjected Anna implying that this was a one off. She cast a doubtful glance in Alice's direction.

"We'll take the Range Rover," said Middlebrook.

Joe hadn't noticed the white 4x4 parked in front of the RV and couldn't help but be impressed by the set up they had here. Middlebrook started up the engine as Joe stepped into the car and Alice watched as the red tail lights disappeared into the dusk.

Whilst clearing the table, Anna noticed her gaze and said, "Don't be getting any ideas. The last thing we need is you complicating things."

"I don't know what you mean," replied Alice with mock indignation.

Smiling, Alice turned and pulled herself up into the RV. She was tired and hungry then realising that Anna had started preparing a meal for her, Alice decided to flop on her bed for a while.

Soon Alice was sitting down at the table heartily digging into a plate of spaghetti whilst Anna sat opposite with a mug of coffee.

"What happened out there?" enquired Anna.

"What do you mean?" replied Alice knowing exactly what she meant.

"That trance you went into when you were saying goodbye to Joe. I've seen it before, at the lakes in England. It happened when you looked at me."

Realising that Anna was not going to be fobbed off Alice decided to tell her as much as she dare.

"I see things," said Alice timidly, "it's almost as if I am there."

"What – what things? Where?" Anna's curiosity was peaked but given Alice's track record she was also apprehensive.

"Just now I saw Joe on a beach but it was weird, he was glowing and there was this strange figure behind him who I couldn't make out."

"And what about me Alice, what did you see then?" Anna was almost afraid to ask.

"I saw you in a hut, I think, you were sat down and holding a baby in each arm. Barny was standing by, looking down at you."

"Two babies," said Anna excitedly, "and that's all."

Alice nodded; she felt it prudent to be economical with the truth. She thought the fact that one of the babies had oversize but human looking eyes might freak Anna out. Anna finally leant back on her chair and shaking her head said, "I don't know Alice ... what are we going to do with you"

* * *

"You'll need to pick up Highway 95 and head north," said Joe as they started to leave the clearing.

"Right," said Middlebrook, "how far up do I need to go?"

"About twenty miles or so – I'll tell you when to turn off."

Joe's curiosity got the better of him; he needed to know more about these people.

"So Mr Middlebrook, what brings you to this part of the world?" he enquired.

"Barnabus please," said Middlebrook, "we've been touring the country – gradually working our way west and this is our latest stop off point."

"How long have you been here?"

"Oh about six months or so." Middlebrook was trying to be as vague as possible. He didn't want to be too secretive however, that would have only aroused unnecessary suspicion. On the other hand he didn't want to give too much away either.

"What is Alice to you and Anna? Is she a niece or something?" asked Joe.

"No," Middlebrook paused for thought, "no she's just a friend," he replied, reluctant to talk about Alice at all.

"She's certainly got spunk I'll give her that," said Joe.

Middlebrook raised his eyebrows at this then remembered that spunk meant spirit or gumption over here. It was true; considering what Alice had been through she had bounced back remarkably well. Middlebrook decided to change the subject.

"Do you live in Sandpoint?"

"No, I live in a small town called Arrow Creek, It's a little ways north of Sandpoint." Still intrigued Joe decided to keep pumping for information. "What do you do for a living?"

"I'm a doctor," replied Middlebrook hoping to leave it at that.

"What field?" pressed Joe, "medicine?"

"Psychiatry," stated Middlebrook bluntly.

"You're a shrink!"

"I suppose," continued Middlebrook, "so is Anna."

"And Alice is she a..." Joe was cut short.

"No – like I said she's just a friend," interrupted Middlebrook.

"What about you?" he continued, "what do you do?" trying to deflect the conversation away from Alice.

"I'm a vet," replied Joe, "plus I'm a sergeant in the National Guard."

They both sat in silence for a while until finally Joe said, "Turn off here, my truck should be less than a quarter of a mile down this track."

Sure enough, very soon a metallic blue Chevy pick-up loomed into the lights. Middlebrook pulled up to a halt and Joe thanked him for the lift.

"And thank you for helping Alice," Middlebrook replied, "I doubt if we will be seeing you again."

Joe shrugged and smiled, "Who knows, anyway be seeing ya Barnab ... I can't call you that, how about Doc?" he said with a grin.

Middlebrook nodded and grinned back. Nice though Joe was, he hoped this would be the last they saw of him, so it didn't really matter.

Turning the car round, Middlebrook headed back. With this encounter he felt events were getting out of his control and that somehow they hadn't seen the last of him.

CHAPTER SIX
YOU'D BETTER BELIEVE IT

The convoy continued on, pitching from side to side as they travelled along the forest track. It was dark now and Alice could barely make out any of the people in her truck. She tried to hold on whilst the truck endeavoured to throw her and the others around.

"This is getting a little uncomfortable," she said.

"We should be getting onto a road soon," replied Joe optimistically.

In the darkness Cardenas asked, "Does anyone know anything about this underground base we are headed for?"

"It's a DUMB you dummy!" exclaimed Katlin provocatively.

"What's a DUMB?" replied Cardenas ignoring her rancour.

Katlin rolled her eyes, she didn't suffer fools gladly. "It stands for Deep Underground Military Base. The government has always denied their existence but it is believed that there are hundreds all over the States."

"One of the most famous is the Dulce base in New Mexico," added Joe, "another is called Mount Weather, and of course there's Area 51 where allegedly something is going on below ground."

"How are we going to get in Joe?" enquired Alice.

"I don't know for sure, I guess that is why General Jackson is coming along for the ride. He must have access."

Alice nodded and the lorry fell silent again. In the darkness she could just about make out Joe's face. She smiled inwardly and thought back to the second time that they met...

* * *

It was a beautiful late spring morning in downtown Arrow Creek. The midday sun seemed to hang overhead pouring warmth and optimism which always seems to arrive at this time of the year.

Walking along Main Street however, Joe was more than a little pre-occupied to notice. Ever since meeting Alice, he just couldn't seem to get her out of his head. Joe's wife, Isobel, had died five years earlier of a brain tumour and he still hadn't got over it. He had had plenty of opportunities to date, Katlin had been especially pushy, but he just wasn't interested. Now much to his surprise, he found himself thinking about this pretty young thing who he rescued from a Grizzly up in the mountains.

Still contemplating his thoughts, Joe unconsciously opened the door to the diner where Katlin worked and stepped in. He walked over to the counter, smiling, as he saw Katlin smiling back with a coffee jug in her hand.

"Hey Joe," she said brightly, "coffee?" knowing exactly what his answer would be.

"Please, and some apple pie, I'm feeling peckish today."

As Katlin organised his order Joe scanned his eyes around the room. All the usual faces were there except one. Sitting on her own by the window was Alice drinking a cup of coffee. Joe turned back to Katlin and asked, "That girl over there by the window, how long has she been here?"

"About twenty minutes I guess. Why, do you know her?" said Katlin a little uneasy.

"Kinda," replied Joe.

"I'm not sure but I think she's Briti..." trailed off Katlin as Joe, not listening, walked over holding his pie and coffee.

Alice, sensing a presence, looked up to see Joe standing at the table. "Oh hello Joe." she smiled.

"Hi," replied Joe smiling back, "mind if I join you?"

"Not at all, take a seat."

Joe sat down and started to tuck into his pie. Alice just watched him and sipped her coffee. Finally, he said, "So what brings you to this neck of the woods?"

"We needed provisions, I was going to drink this and head back."

"Lucky I came in when did then or I might have missed you," said Joe surprised at his own candour. "How is your ankle by the way?"

"I suppose," replied Alice with a little more caution, "my ankle's much better now thanks." She too had been thinking a lot about Joe but wasn't going to make the fact obvious. "Actually I'm glad we bumped into each other," she continued, "I want to ask you something."

"Okay."

"Will you teach me to shoot properly. Barny said that you are a member of the National Guard. So you must be pretty good."

"Yeah I'm a pretty good shot," replied Joe feeling slightly flattered.

Before he could answer Alice's question Katlin arrived with a coffee pot in her hand. She had been watching their conversation from behind the counter and didn't much like what she saw.

"Top up anyone?" said Katlin with an overly cheerful tone.

Alice glanced up to see the waitress who had served her earlier. Katlin was about Alice's height but much slimmer. Her face had slightly more pointed features, framed by short, jet black hair. She was of Irish extraction which probably accounted for her feisty nature.

Joe knew exactly why Katlin had come over. For some time now she had made it clear to Joe that she liked him but he had always held her at arm's length, not because he didn't like her, he just wasn't interested in general. Now it seemed that Katlin saw Alice as some kind of threat.

"Aren't you going to introduce me?" asked Katlin.

"Oh – right," replied Joe, "Alice this is my good friend Katlin."

Alice and Katlin shook hands and sized each other up.

"You kept her quiet Joe," said Katlin, "where did you two meet?"

"It was only a few days ago, up in the mountains."

"Well," said Alice, "it's time I was heading back. Nice to meet you Katlin." Alice stood up to go and Joe stood up also. As Alice started to walk out of the diner Joe said goodbye to Katlin and followed Alice into the street.

"I didn't give you an answer," said Joe catching up with Alice.

She looked at him expectantly.

"How about this Saturday, I know a range that we can use?"

"That sounds great – where shall we meet?" enquired Alice.

"How about here at 10am,"

"Fine," said Alice smiling, "I'll see you here then."

Opening the door to the Range Rover, Alice got in and drove off. Joe watched the car disappear down the street and wondered what he had started.

* * *

The Range Rover pulled up in front of the diner on Saturday morning and Alice switched off the engine and banged the steering wheel in frustration. She was angry and upset after having a row with Middlebrook and Anna over getting involved with Joe. They didn't want her to go but knew that there was little that they could do to stop her. Alice's argument was that there was going to come a point when other people would have to get involved, and if it had to be someone then why not a person with connections to the National Guard. The argument resulted in Alice storming out, leaving Middlebrook and Anna exasperated knowing that nothing had been resolved.

Alice stepped out of the car and looked around her. She was fifteen minutes early and Joe was nowhere to be seen. As Alice leant against the car, Katlin appeared, she had seen Alice arrive and decided to go out and confront her.

"Oh, hello," said Alice, "Err Katlin isn't it?"

Katlin looked Alice up and down; her manner was clearly not friendly.

"Who are you?" she said rhetorically, "you stroll in from God knows where and think you can take what you want."

Alice instinctively knew that Katlin was talking about Joe; it was obvious the day before that Katlin was showing signs of jealousy.

"We're just friends," replied Alice, "there's no need to get all possessive."

Katlin lunged towards Alice and pushed her forearm against her throat, pressing Alice against the car.

"Friends," said Katlin with contempt in her voice, "Joe and me have been friends for years. So if you know what's good for you – back off."

Suddenly Joe's pick-up pulled into the diner and Katlin released her hold on Alice. As Joe got out and walked over to the girls, he sensed that something was going on.

"Is everything okay here?" he enquired.

"Everything is just fine," replied Katlin, "we were just getting acquainted." She turned and glared at Alice to see her reaction.

"Yes," confirmed a ruffled Alice, "just passing the time of day."

Joe didn't believe a word of it but decided to let it go for the time being.

"Right Alice, if you follow me in your jeep we can get started," said Joe opening the door to his truck. Alice nodded and got into her car. As they drove off Alice noticed Katlin staring from the diner doorway. She couldn't believe what had just happened and was annoyed with herself for allowing Katlin to intimidate her so easily.

After a short drive, they eventually arrived at the firing range and in no time Joe was putting Alice through her paces. Alice determined to improve was attentive and eager to learn and showed definite signs of improvement very quickly. Eventually Joe went to his pick-up and returned with a semi-automatic rifle.

"Let's see how you do with a proper weapon." he said with a smile.

Alice took the rifle and while still standing took aim at the target. She pulled the trigger and let go a short burst of rounds. The bull's eye of the target was peppered with bullet holes. Alice turned to Joe with a big grin on her face. Joe nodded his approval.

"Not bad, you seem to have taken to that no problem."

"We have a rifle similar to this back at the camp; I shall practise with it."

Joe nodded in reply. He had forgotten about the small cache of weapons he'd seen in the RV – it troubled him but decided to say nothing until he knew her better.

"I suppose I ought to be getting back," said Alice with a sigh. Then after pausing for thought she asked, "Do you know any self-defence moves at all?"

"Well we are taught hand-to-hand combat as part of our training."

"Could you teach me?" asked Alice again almost apologetically, "I know that I'm taking up a lot of your time."

Joe didn't mind, he was enjoying Alice's company. She was intense but in a different way to Katlin – less in your face. He was finding himself more and more attracted to her but wasn't sure whether he was just being used.

"Sure – how about tomorrow," he replied, then hastily added, "if you're not doing anything."

"No not at all – tomorrow will be fine. What time?"

"How about elevenish at my place; we can use my garage to train in."

"I'll need directions to your house," said a beaming Alice.

Joe drew a map on a scrap of paper and handed it to her.

"Thank you so much Joe," said Alice, "'til tomorrow then."

With that she gave him a peck on the cheek, got into her car and drove off. Her encounter with Katlin earlier in the day made Alice realise that she had to toughen up and learn how to defend herself.

* * *

That evening over dinner, Alice announced her intention to go over to Joe's the next day. The atmosphere from the morning's argument was a little tense and Alice was expecting another fight. To her surprise however they just nodded resignedly.

"You are your own woman," said Middlebrook, "you must do what you think is best."

"Why don't you like him?" asked Alice.

"It's not that we don't like him," added Anna, "We don't know him. It's a matter of trust."

"Well we need to start trusting people soon," stated Alice, "we can't fight this war on our own."

Middlebrook had to concede; Alice was right on this but what he feared more than anything at this point was ridicule. After all, who was going to believe such a crazy story?

Late Sunday morning Alice arrived at Joe's house. She walked up to the door and knocked. Joe came to the door wearing camouflage trousers and jacket. He smiled and beckoned her in. Alice took off her coat – she was wearing tracksuit trousers and a sweatshirt.

"Would you like a drink?" offered Joe.

"No thanks, let's get started."

Joe showed Alice through to the double garage where he had laid down some gym mats.

"I'm going to take you through some basic moves first of all, just to warm up."

During the next two hours, Joe demonstrated self-defence moves from the front and behind: how to disable an armed attacker, and more. Alice picked it up very quickly to the point where eventually she was anticipating Joe's moves and throwing him to the ground almost every time.

After one final drop to the ground Joe was lying on his back. Alice stood over him straddling his waist. Then she dropped down almost sitting on Joe and pinned his shoulders to the floor.

"Enough already," said Joe," I give in." He was hot and sweating and noticed Alice was too. Joe extricated himself out from underneath Alice. "I'm going for a shower," he said, as he started to make his way to the bathroom.

"I'll follow in after you," replied Alice still panting a little.

Joe stepped into the steaming shower cubicle and started to soap himself down. Suddenly he heard the door slide open. He turned around to see Alice naked, stepping into the shower with a big smile on her face. Noticing Joe's surprise she said, "Well I did say that I would follow you in."

* * *

The grey mist swirled around Alice's body as she lay seemingly suspended in mid-air. It felt to her as though the mist itself was supporting her. She opened her eyes and tried to focus. She could just about discern shadowy figures moving about inside the mist. Eventually one of the figures moved closer until Alice could clearly see the creature standing before her. It was a Deviant, slim and slight, wearing a black skin tight suit that revealed her figure; the small breasts betraying the fact that she was clearly female. Her head was shaved bald except for a red and blue pony tail set high on her crown sticking up, arching over and cascading down her back. The large almond shaped eyes were black, shiny and lifeless. Alice looked up at her, terrified, but unable to move. With a slight grin on her face the Deviant brought a knife round from behind her back. It was broad, eight and a half inches long and razor sharp. She placed the tip on the right hand side of Alice's abdomen and pushed down. Blood welled out of the wound and Alice tried to scream but no sound came out. Then, with a large grin on her face, the Deviant pulled the knife across her abdomen to the left leaving an incision ten inches long and oozing blood. Pulling the knife out of the wound, the Deviant held the blade vertically to her mouth with the edge to her lips. Blood from the knife ran down the handle and over her hand. She looked at Alice and grinned again then stuck out her tongue – it was slightly forked, with a prong on each side of the knife blade – then she ran the knife slowly down, licking the blood off at the same time.

Alice sat bolt upright in bed and shook Joe violently out of his doze.

"What is it?" he said shocked and confused, "what's happening?"

"It's alright," replied Alice still reeling from the nightmare.

She lay back down and snuggled into Joe still panting slightly. "I was dreaming that's all, I must have dozed off."

"Some dream," said Joe, "what was it about?"

"I can't remember," Alice lied; she remembered the dream vividly but didn't want to explain it to Joe. How could she.

Snuggling closer to Joe, Alice felt him put his arm around her and they lay there quietly for a while until Joe broke the silence.

"Alice I couldn't help but notice the scars on your left wrist. Do you want to tell me about them?"

Alice looked at her wrist, she had forgotten about the scars. They were still slightly red, giving away the fact that they were fairly recent. She hastily put her left arm under the sheets in a pointless attempt to hide them.

"You can talk to me you know," said Joe, "I won't think any the less of you."

Alice thought for a while and then realised that she was going to have to tell him something. She turned to him and said, "For a while last year I went a little crazy; Barny insists that I was more severely traumatised but I felt as though I was going crazy at the time."

"What caused it?" asked Joe more intrigued than ever.

Suddenly moving to the edge of the bed Alice leant to the floor, picked up some clothes and pulled her sports bra on. Looking back at Joe she smiled and said, "shall I make us something to eat?"

By now it was mid-afternoon and she was hungry.

"Sure – why not," replied Joe not wanting to press Alice any further, she obviously wasn't ready yet. He was hungry also and it had been a while since a woman had cooked for him.

Rummaging around in Joe's half empty fridge Alice pulled out some eggs, an onion and some mushrooms.

"How about an omelette," she shouted back to the bedroom assuming that Joe was getting dressed.

Joe was only a few steps behind her wearing only a T-shirt and boxer shorts. Alice had put on one of his shirts and he couldn't help but notice how sexy she looked.

"That will be fine," said Joe walking up behind her, putting his arms around her waist and giving her a peck on the cheek.

Shortly they were sitting down to eat. Joe was hungry and ate his omelette with gusto, while Alice ate some, and then started playing with her food, deep in thought.

"It's not that I don't want to tell you," she said eventually, knowing that she was going to have to say something, "it's just that if I told you what happened, you really would think I'm crazy."

"Try me," replied Joe, and leant back on his chair to gauge her reaction.

Alice sighed, and decided she was going to tell him everything.

For the next half hour or so Joe listened intently to Alice's story. From the day she told her husband John that she was pregnant right up to the point where they met in the mountains.

"Well that's it," Alice said eventually. "You know everything now."

Joe sat opposite her in stunned silence. It was one of the most insane stories he'd ever heard.

After a while he said, "You can't expect me to believe that, I'd have to be…"

"Mad?" interjected Alice indignantly. She got up and stormed into the bedroom. By the time Joe walked into the bedroom Alice was fully dressed.

"What are you doing?" asked Joe frowning.

"Get dressed," demanded Alice, "I'm taking you back to our camp."

Joe started to get dressed, when he heard a knock on the door.

"I'll get it," said Alice still in an angry tone, "you finish getting your clothes on."

Opening the door Alice was confronted with Katlin whose smile changed instantly to a frown. Alice walked out of the house a few steps and said, "What are you doing here?"

"More to the point," snapped Katlin, "what the hell are you doing here?"

With that she pushed Alice against the house. Alice was ready for her this time however, and grabbed Katlin's right arm and swung her round pushing her face against the wall. Alice was still angry at Joe's reaction and was more than happy to take it out on Katlin. Alice had Katlin's arm behind her back and pushed it up towards her shoulder blade.

"You're hurting me." cried Katlin.

"That's the last time you lay a finger on me – is that clear," snarled Alice.

Katlin didn't reply immediately so Alice pushed her arm up further.

"Okay, okay," Katlin grimaced, "now let me go."

Releasing her grip, Alice watched as Katlin tried to regain her composure. At this point Joe came to the door.

"Who's at the door, Alice?" Looking round he saw Katlin. "Oh – hi Katlin, what brings you round here?"

"Just a social call," replied a still flustered Katlin. It wasn't – Katlin suspected that something was going on between them and came round to see if they were together. Her fears were confirmed.

"Unfortunately we've got things to do now so I'll just have to take a rain check on that," Joe continued, he had barely noticed her demeanour, "I'll drop into the diner tomorrow."

Katlin nodded, and still angry, as much with herself for letting that Limey get the better of her, got into her car and drove home.

"Why are we going to your place?" enquired Joe.

"Just shut up and follow me. You'll see."

Joe and Alice got into their respective cars and drove off towards the camp, Joe wondering what the hell was going on.

* * *

On the drive over, Joe's thoughts turned to his wife. He had just made love to the first woman since she had died five years ago and now he was feeling guilty. He knew his feelings were irrational but couldn't help himself; their relationship had been a good one and he still missed her. Now he seemed to be getting in deeper with a girl who was driving faster than he felt comfortable with and worse, showing signs of being somewhat unstable.

Speeding along as fast as she dare, Alice was concerned that Joe might change his mind and turn back. She was fully aware of how insane her story sounded to Joe. She knew that he was going to have to know sooner or later so why not get it over with. Alice was desperate to get him to the camp to show him the only proof that they had.

Anna and Middlebrook had just finished eating an alfresco dinner and were enjoying a glass of wine in the late-afternoon sun when two vehicles turned into the clearing. They both turned and looked at each other in surprise. Why was Alice bringing Joe back? Alice stepped out of the car and walked purposefully up to the table – Joe following behind, deliberately holding back.

"Hi Alice," said Middlebrook cautiously, he could see something was amiss, "hello Joe."

Alice ignored the greeting; her mind was focused on one thing. "Barny, I've told him everything!" she announced.

"Oh that's just great," said Anna showing her displeasure. She glared at Alice and stormed into the RV. Middlebrook on the other hand sat trying to keep his composure.

"Was that wise?" he said finally.

"People are going to have to find out eventually and … well I trust him," blurted out Alice.

Middlebrook turned his attention to Joe. "And what do you make of all this Joe?"

Joe shrugged his shoulders and before he could reply Alice placed her hands on the table to get closer and said to Middlebrook, "Show him the DVD, Barny, it's the only proof we have."

Middlebrook sighed with exasperation and gave it some thought. Realising that he had little choice and that there was nothing to be gained now by hiding the proof, Middlebrook stepped into the RV to get his laptop. Returning he set the laptop down on the table, inserted the DVD and let it run.

"Did Alice tell you about the storage device?" asked Middlebrook.

"Yes," said Joe, "she didn't say you had a copy though."

"I managed to download it before the device was taken from me."

By now the DVD had started and all three watched intensely. Joe stared at the strange creature on the screen incredulously as it imparted its dire warning. When the DVD finally came to an end Joe sat down, he turned to Middlebrook.

"This is a joke right? It's got to be some elaborate hoax."

"It's no hoax Joe," replied Middlebrook, "I wish it was."

"Shouldn't the government know about this?" he continued.

"They do!" said Alice and Middlebrook in unison.

"I'm sure our government would have informed yours," added Middlebrook, "and a few other countries besides."

"What are they doing about it?" asked a visibly alarmed Joe.

"What can they do," replied Middlebrook, "we don't know when or where they will attack, and besides with their technology I suspect that we are pretty much defenceless anyway."

Middlebrook paused to let this sink in until finally Joe stood up and said, "No, I can't take all this in. It can't be happening." He got his car keys out of his pocket. "I've gotta go," he said a little calmer. As he made his way over to his pick-up Alice sidled up to him.

"Don't go like this."

He could see that she was close to tears. "I'll see you soon," he said, not knowing for sure whether he was being honest or not.

Just then Anna came to the door of the RV, she looked ashen. "You might want to come and see this," she said, "all of you."

They all stepped into the RV and Anna pointed at the television and said, "Look."

They all turned to look at the TV and to their astonishment they could see a giant orb about one hundred feet in diameter. It was matt black with slightly raised patterns on its surface and appeared to be hovering some ten feet off the ground. The orb had materialised in front of the White House and was hovering partly over The Ellipse Park and Constitution Avenue – the Washington Memorial could be seen behind it. Panicking drivers were screeching to a halt causing collisions and chaos on the road.

Watching transfixed they listened to what the reporter had to say.

"Suddenly appearing in front of the White House minutes ago and nobody seems to know what it is or what it's doing here."

"I've just switched on," said Anna, "It's on all the channels."

"What the hell is it!" exclaimed Joe.

They continued to listen to the reporter who was speaking from a helicopter circling the orb.

"We are just getting reports in that thousands of these giant balls have appeared in strategic points all over the planet. No official statement has be…"

The broadcast was suddenly interrupted by a yellow beam emanating from the orb and the TV screen went blank.

Alice turned to look at Middlebrook and said, "It's started Barny. It's starting at last." She then moved over to Joe and held him close. Joe continued to look at the television which had just come back on showing the giant orb from ground level. "Do you believe me now?" said Alice, looking up at Joe.

Joe looked at the screen – he saw it but still couldn't believe it.

CHAPTER SEVEN
SPHERES OF DESTINY

The President of the United States of America stood up from behind his desk in the oval office, looked out of the window again and without saying a word started to make his way out of the room. He was followed by the vice president and four Secret Service agents. Walking hurriedly through the west wing and into the central hall, he finally entered the oval drawing room which led out onto the Truman Balcony. From there they could clearly see beyond the South Lawn, this gave him an ideal view of the massive sphere which had been hovering over the far end of The Ellipse and Constitution Avenue. It had been there for over two minutes now and nothing had happened.

"Mr. President, I think it's time to get you to safety," said an increasingly nervous Secret Service agent, "we're a little exposed up here."

A helicopter suddenly flew into view distracting them and was flying around the sphere. They watched as a thin yellow beam shot out of the sphere and hit the helicopter which exploded in a ball of fire. As burning debris was falling out of the sky, small pin pricks of blue light appeared all over the surface of the sphere. The lights grew larger in diameter until they started to merge and eventually form a continuous blue haze over the entire surface. After showing clear aggression a force field had just been deployed.

The group heard a noise coming in from the east, it was a lone Lockheed Martin F35a fighter – it barely got close before another thin yellow beam of light shot out of the sphere and destroyed the fighter. As it crashed just inside the White House grounds, they watched as scattered debris burned on the well-manicured lawns.

"It's time to go, sir," said the agent, this time with slight panic in his voice.

There was no delay, everyone made their way into the building and eventually down to the basement.

"Where are our families?" asked the president.

"They're already in the P.E.O.C.," replied one of the agents, "they are safe. The vice president's family are on their way down now."

The president frowned but said nothing. He doubted whether anyone was safe. Was this building going to become their tomb?

* * *

From the President's Emergency Operations Center, a vigil was kept on the sphere. For the rest of the evening and night it simply hovered motionless doing nothing.

Soldiers had assembled in front of the building nervously keeping guard with guns pointed directly at the sphere.

The president arrived in the basement and was taken directly to his worried family who were billeted in a separate room. He tried to comfort them and then made his way into the main ops room. There he saw a group of officers talking and shaking their heads.

"Excuse me gentlemen," he said, "what's the status, and please, don't sugar coat it."

The highest ranking officer in the group, Colonel Robert Peterson, felt it his place to answer the president and give him the bad news.

"Well, sir," he said with a sigh, "these spheres are all over the country – all over the planet in fact. They are placed in strategic locations to the point where the whole planet is in lockdown."

"Have we no defence? I saw one fighter try to make an attack."

"That was the only aircraft that managed to take off. All the others were destroyed on the ground," commented Peterson. "We have no army to speak of, no air force, our missile silos have been neutralised, not that we could use them anyway. We can't nuke our own country."

"And Air Force One?"

"Destroyed on the ground also." Peterson saw a cloud come over the president's face.

At that moment it suddenly went dark and seconds later the lights came back on again.

"What was that?" enquired the startled president.

"They have just cut off our main power supply. The back-up generator has just kicked in."

"Are we getting out of here Bob?" The president's expression was almost pleading.

Peterson had little comfort for him but decided to be diplomatic. "I honestly don't know, sir, it's not looking good."

"I'll be with my family, let me know if there are any developments."

With that the president walked away and as he entered the family room, he glanced at his wife who was looking with a worried expectant expression. In reply he gave her a very slight shake of the head that told her that the situation was desperate.

* * *

An hour after the sun had risen over the horizon the next day, there came a loud metallic crack and then a creaking sound.

A soldier in the ops room was sent to summon the president, who was trying, with little success to get some sleep with his family.

"Something's happening, sir," he said excitedly, "you might want to see this."

The president followed the soldier into the ops room where several large screens displayed the grounds outside. The sphere appeared to be opening. Four sections on the side facing the White House were sliding slowly into the rear part. Steadily the four curved triangular sections got smaller until finally all that could be seen was a flat shimmering vertical blue surface. There was a pause for about a minute and the tension in the ops room was palpable.

Suddenly from the outer perimeter of the sphere came a blue light similar to the force field. The circular beam, the same diameter as the sphere, shot across the lawns at rapid speed until it hit the main entrance of the White House blasting a hole in the wall and roof. The pillars of the South Portico shattered and the roof they were supporting crumbled and fell to the ground around the beam. A few soldiers that were in its way were instantly vaporised. Others, who were close, were knocked off their feet and blown sideways, some being crushed by falling masonry. In the ops room everyone looked up nervously as they felt the building shake with the impact.

As all the personnel watched apprehensively at the screens, two shadowy images hurtled at speed inside the beam.

"What's that?" asked the president.

"It looks as though that beam is hollow, I think it was some kind of vessel," stated Peterson. "I suspect we are about to meet our visitors."

* * *

The leading vessel entered the White House on the first floor through the shattered wall and settled, hovering low in the blue room. Immediately it was met with a hail of machine gun fire from agents and the few soldiers that were left on the first floor. The bullets had no effect however, merely bouncing off the outer shell of the shiny metallic gold surface.

In the smaller vessel hovering close behind, Commander-In-Chief DM Khai Drypha observed the activity. He expected resistance but still viewed it as an inconvenience. He was tall and slim with short, cropped white hair like most of his people, and had an air of confidence and arrogance that made him at ease in his position of command. His uniform was simple – dark grey trousers and jacket and the sleeves had insignia picked out in red.

"Neutralise them quickly," he said turning to his second in command, "I want this building secured as soon as possible."

His second in command was female, shorter and slight. Her head was shaved with a shock of red and blue hair draped down her back in a ponytail. HT Mida Raar simply smiled and gave an order into a microphone by her left cheek.

"Blast them," she ordered.

Inside the blue room there came a loud high pitched noise emanating from the first vessel. The defenders immediately dropped their weapons and held their hands over their ears. Many dropped to the floor in agony, blood streaming down from their nose and ears.

The noise stopped and a side door opened on the leading vessel and several Deviant solders – Nih-troopers – ran down and made their way over to the incapacitated personnel. One by one they were picked off by the Nih-troopers with a single laser shot to the heart. Once the blue room was secured the Nih-troopers fanned out into the other rooms in a bid to secure the whole building. A fierce battle ensued as they infiltrated the entrance hall, with army soldiers trying to defend from the North Portico. The soldiers were dispatched quickly with only a few Nih-trooper casualties. As the troops made their way through each room, two troopers entered the family dining room. It appeared to be empty, but just as they were about to leave one of them heard a slight noise coming from the pantry.

"Wait," said one. He put his finger up to his lips to hush his partner and then pointed to an opening which led to the pantry. Carefully they made their way to the gap and furtively looked in. Cowering at the far end was a man in his mid-thirties and a girl in her early twenties. They were both wearing suits and it was obvious that they were non-combatants.

"Don't shoot, please," pleaded the man. "We are unarmed."

The girl stood motionless transfixed with fear.

The first Nih-trooper started to raise his gun to take aim but the second trooper stayed his arm and shook his head.

"No," he said firmly, "take them – they may be of use."

The two prisoners were hustled out into the blue room where by now Khai Drypha and Mida Raar were surveying the chaos and destruction.

Pushing the prisoners in front of them one of the troopers said, "We found them hiding, sir; I thought they may be of some use."

"Good," replied Drypha, "let's get them out of this mayhem."

The prisoners were man handled into the East Room to be interrogated.

The room was large and empty except for a grand piano and stool which stood in one corner.

Drypha stopped for a few seconds to admire the room's elegance, before returning to the matter in hand. Mida, having no interest in such things, already had her laser gun pointing at the man.

"No," he said to Mida putting his hand on her forearm to make her lower her gun, "there's no need for any unpleasantness. At least not yet."

"Wha – what do you want," stammered the man.

"What's your name?" enquired Drypha.

"Brian," came the terrified reply.

"Well Brian," continued Drypha in an unsettlingly calm voice, "do you know where we can find the president?"

"No, I don't know where he is."

Mida moved closer raising her gun again.

"Are you sure?" said Drypha sounding a little more threatening now "Your life might depend on it."

"For God's sake tell him," screamed the girl. It was as much as she could take.

"And what's your name?" asked Drypha turning his attention to the girl.

"Kellie," stammered the girl, tears streaming down her face.

"You can go to hell," said Brian summoning all the courage he had left, "fuck you – you won't get away with this."

"I think you will find that we already have," said Mida close in his ear.

Turning to Mida, Drypha simply nodded his head. She raised her gun and shot a beam. It hit the wall just to the right of Brian's neck. Brian smiled in relief, he couldn't believe that she could miss from such close range. Mida smiled back mischievously, and then whipped the beam across his neck. Nothing happened for a second then Brian's eyes rolled up into his head. His body slumped back, slid down the wall to the floor while his head fell forwards and dropped with dull thump on the carpet. There was very little blood, the laser had cauterised the wound as it made its incision. Mida picked up the severed head by the hair and held it twelve inches from Kellie's face. She looked in horror at the white eyes and could faintly smell burnt flesh. Wetting her trousers, she wanted to scream but nothing came out except a muted gurgle.

"Now Kellie, do *you* know where I can find the president?" Drypha was calm but beginning to lose his patience.

"Yes – yes he's in the basement room," stammered Kellie, "but it's secure, you won't get in."

"Don't you trouble yourself over that," replied Mida.

"Can you show us?" enquired Drypha.

Kellie nodded and as they started to leave the East Room a Nih-trooper approached and said, "The building is secure, sir."

"Excellent," smiled Drypha, "assemble your men, we are heading for the basement."

* * *

"They're in here," said Kellie, pointing at the large steel door that led into the ops room. "They won't open the door, even if you threaten to kill me," she continued nervously.

Drypha smiled at her and said, "That won't be necessary."

Pointing at the camera above the door he said, "Destroy it."

Mida took aim and blasted the camera off the wall.

A Nih-trooper walked up to the door with a large rectangular tablet, pressed a few buttons and held it up to the wall.

"What can you see?" asked Drypha.

The tablet showed several orange silhouettes moving around. By scanning the tablet across the wall the trooper was able to get a good idea of how many were in the room and which ones were armed.

"Approximately thirty, sir, about half of them are armed – small weapons. There is another room that I think has non-military personnel in it."

"Let's get this door down," said Drypha.

A piece of apparatus was brought up and placed about four feet from the door. Everyone, including Kellie, were given ear defenders. Then a trooper holding a remote further down the corridor pressed a button.

Instantly a loud boom sounded and a powerful blast knocked the door inwards where it crashed with a hefty thud. Two soldiers inside the room, who were close to the door with guns ready, were crushed by the force.

Instantly a protective shield shot up from the apparatus. It was a faint green in colour but still allowed the invaders to see through it. The inhabitants of the room looked curiously at the Deviants as though they were behind a water tank.

Drypha could see the ops room personnel clearly also. He turned to a trooper and said, "Kill a few."

The Nih-trooper shot three times through the screen, killing three men.

A number of men returned fire but the bullets hit the screen and were absorbed by it, suspended as if in some kind of gel.

"Shoot!" commanded Drypha.

Nih- troopers stood across the width of the door and returned fire through the screen. Seven armed men and one unarmed woman, caught in the cross fire, lay dead in the room.

The president, watching from the side, saw the carnage unfold. Appalled, he walked into the middle of the room and said, "Stop, put down your weapons. We can't fight them, it's useless."

A few men showed reluctance and looked at each other.

"I order you to put them down," asserted the president, "this stops here."

A Nih-trooper turned to Drypha and said, "They've put down their weapons."

The screen was switched off and Drypha ordered several troopers to make their way into the room.

He and Mida followed behind. Troopers fanned out and stood side by side, weapons poised ready. Drypha made his way to the centre of the line.

"It's time that I introduced myself," said Drypha with an air of pomposity,

"I am DM Khai Drypha, Commander- In- Chief of this invasion force."

The president stepped forward to make himself known. "I am the Pres…"

"Yes I know who you are," interrupted Drypha, "we have been watching your time period for years."

"Why are you here?" said the exasperated president. "What do you want?"

"What do we want?" repeated Drypha for effect. He smiled. "Everything – we want everything you have."

Some Nih-troopers had been sent in to gather every-one together and one trooper was dragging a hysterical young girl by the arm. Her mother was shouting and protesting whilst being restrained by troopers.

The president made a move to try and release the girl but three troopers blocked his way. "Leave her, that's my daughter," he cried. The girl was an attractive nineteen year old with long blonde hair.

"Take her into the corridor," said Drypha. The girl was led away screaming and struggling to no avail.

"You'll rot in hell for this," hissed the president.

Mida, wanting to make her presence known, came forward. "We know all about your petty superstitions – they mean nothing to us."

Turning his back on the president, Drypha looked at Mida with a smile and said, "There's nothing here of any consequence. Kill them – kill them all."

As he walked into the corridor he could hear laser guns firing off behind him. Shortly Mida came back into the corridor with the Nih-troopers following behind.

"The planet has been secured in less than two days," said Mida bristling with pride.

"There is some military activity though – regions of potential resistance," said Drypha thoughtfully, "particularly in the north-west – I believe they call it Idaho. I want you to go there, isolate and eliminate it. The teleportation network is operational now – use it."

"What about these two?" said Mida, gesturing towards the two girls.

"They are good specimens," observed Drypha, "put them with the others."

Mida simply nodded and left.

Drypha ordered the two girls to be removed and as they were escorted away, Kellie said in a trembling voice, "You're not going to kill us are you?"

Drypha said nothing but he thought: *No, but soon you'll wish we had*.

* * *

Early Monday morning Alice awoke with a start. The sun was shining and birds were chirping noisily. Alice got up and decided to make herself a cup of tea; she was fed up with coffee, and wanted something that reminded her of home. Feeling decidedly homesick, her thoughts turned to her parents and she wondered how they were coping with the current situation. She even gave some thought to John and wondered how he was doing. Eventually her thoughts turned to the previous evening when Joe finally realised that everything she had told him was true. His reaction was not what she had expected.

"Damn you for bringing this here," was all he said, before storming out and going home. Alice was dismayed and angry – his attitude simply wasn't fair.

Later that morning whilst the other two were putting lunch on the table, Middlebrook said, "Look we need to decide what we are going to do. Stay here or move on. It seems like we are on our own." The other two shrugged as neither seemed to know what to do for the best.

By mid-afternoon all three were at a low ebb, when suddenly a drab olive green pick-up drove into the clearing followed by two army trucks. Alice didn't recognise it at first and then realised that it was Joe's pick-up hastily repainted. The vehicles pulled up in the centre of the clearing and Joe got out and walked over to the table where Middlebrook, Anna and Alice were sitting. Alice's emotions were in turmoil, she was pleased and relieved to see him but she was still very angry. Standing up, she made a move towards the RV.

"Wait," pleaded Joe, "please I want to talk to you, let me explain."

Alice turned and gave him a look devoid of expression and unconsciously folded her arms in an act of repressed anger.

"I'm sorry about what I said yesterday," he said with as much sincerity as he could muster, "I was wrong – it must have been the shock of realising that what you said was true."

Joe paused to gauge her reaction, Alice stood poker face for a few seconds. He deserved to suffer a little and then eventually gave him a slight smile.

He looked at Middlebrook and Anna, "Can you forgive me?"

Middlebrook relieved that they were no longer alone, gestured over to the soldiers, one of them Katlin, clambering out of the two trucks, "I see you've brought some friends with you."

"They are National Guard, nineteen personnel in all, two trucks and my pick-up," replied Joe, "and some weapons and ammo."

"What have you done to your car?" enquired Alice, her anger subsiding.

"Camouflage of course," replied Joe, pleased that Alice was at least talking to him. "I've got some green paint in the back of my car, and we're going to do the same to your white Range Rover, it sticks out like a sore thumb."

The rest of the day the soldiers busied themselves putting up tents and camouflage awnings to cover the vehicles. Katlin mucked in with the troops but kept a weather eye on Joe and Alice as they masked up the 4x4 and started painting it; their body language and laughter clearly indicating the fondness that they had for each other.

"It's as though they haven't a care in the world," she said to the soldier working with her.

"Cut them some slack, things are gonna change around here pretty soon," said the soldier, failing to pick up on her jealousy.

Later that evening while the soldiers were eating, Middlebrook asked Joe about food rations. "We've got enough for a few days but obviously we are going to need more."

Alice approached Joe and said, "Where are you sleeping tonight?"

"I haven't given it any thought," talking in a mock innocent tone.

"Is that right?" said Alice seeing through him, "well mister you have a lot of making up to do." Taking his hand, she led him to the RV. Anna looked up at Middlebrook dubiously.

"It's none of our business," he said, "she's a grown woman – it's up to her."

Middlebrook's reasoning was, with all the misery that Alice had suffered recently, why not let her have a little joy in her life.

* * *

Early on Wednesday morning Alice woke up to the gentle rhythmic breathing of Joe lying beside her. It was still dark so she squinted at the clock by her bed and saw the time was 5.40am. Sun up was only half an hour away, so she gently slipped out of bed and made her way to the bathroom. After quietly picking up her clothes, she dressed, grabbed a bottle of orange juice from the fridge and made her way outside to the Range Rover. Again very quietly she opened the tail gate to make sure that the rifle and binoculars, which she had put there the night before, were still present.

The previous night, Alice and Joe had had a disagreement. Being frustrated by the fact that they were not doing anything, Alice threatened to go off on her own to do a reconnaissance to see what was happening. Joe was against it, feeling that it was just too risky. The argument ended unresolved, so Alice thought, *to hell with it, I'll go out on my own.*

As she started the car and made her way to the exit, Joe and Middlebrook woke up. Two sentries on the exit tried to challenge her but she was driving too fast and very soon was heading down the track, which lead to the road. Joe stumbled out of the RV half dressed with Middlebrook close behind him. The two guards ran up to him to report what happened.

"What the hell does she think she's doing!" exclaimed Middlebrook.

"She's gone on a fact finding mission." said an exasperated Joe.

"Should we go after her, do you think?"

"No," replied Joe succinctly. "It's too dangerous to have us chasing her all over the region. I'm afraid, for the moment, Alice is on her own."

The sky was overcast when it finally became light forty minutes later. Alice scanned up and down the road, which lead to Arrow Creek. There were no cars, no people, nothing. There was usually some activity at this time of the morning and it seemed as though she was the only living thing around. Eventually she drove into the main street of Arrow Creek, the whole area was deserted. Turning into the carpark of a supermarket, she switched off the engine, picked up her rifle and walked over to the entrance. Peering through the glass she could see it was closed but more than that the whole place seemed shut down. Lifting the rifle, she slammed the butt down on the glass. Nothing happened, so she repeated her action several times until the glass finally gave way and left a hole that Alice could walk through. She expected an alarm to go off but there appeared to be no power. Immediately Alice set about stocking the 4x4 with supplies, mostly tin cans, some fresh vegetables, pre-packed meat and bottled water. When she was satisfied that the 4x4 was full, Alice started the car and made her way out of town to head for higher ground. A quarter of a mile out of town she noticed a wooden house with a veranda, and there sitting quietly on a rocking chair was an old lady. Alice stopped abruptly and stepped out of the 4x4. The lady had a blanket over her lap and a rifle to hand leaning against the wall. Initially she put her hand to the gun but seeing that the stranger was unarmed, relaxed.

"Hello," said Alice brightly as she stepped up onto the veranda, "are you here on our own."

"Yes dear," said the lady, "I've been here own my own for fifteen years now."

"What's your name?" enquired Alice.

"Alice,"

"What a coincidence, my name is Alice too," she chuckled.

The lady looked at least in her mid-eighties and very frail. Her eyes were bright however indicating that her mind was sharper than her looks suggested.

"Alice you can't stay here, everyone has gone."

"Yes," she replied, "They skedaddled out of here a few days ago. I watched them leave."

"Why don't you come with me, it's not safe here."

"Honey," she said, smiling kindly at Alice, "I've lived here for fifty-nine years now. My husband – God rest his soul – built this house. We raised our two boys here. I can't leave. No, if I am going to die it's going to be here surrounded by my memories and the things I love."

Perturbed by the her stubbornness, Alice said goodbye and made her way back to the car, she smiled one last time, waved goodbye and headed off to the mountain tracks.

Soon Alice was heading up a track which led into the hills and woodland. From there under cover she could survey the land over a large area and get some idea of what was happening. The track that she was driving up levelled off and took her through woodland. The clouds were burning off by now and shafts of sunlight were beginning to stream through the branches. Eventually the track opened up on one side and Alice could see the low ground below. It was a good vantage point, so she parked up and grabbed her binoculars. Alice scanned the land, gradually working her way to the horizon. There seemed to be very little activity close by, but in the distance, several plumes of black smoke were drifting into the upper atmosphere. Realising all of a sudden that she was hungry, Alice walked back to the car to find something to eat.

Whilst she was munching on a chocolate brownie, there came a low rumble down the track the way she had come. The rumble got louder and it was obvious that vehicles were coming down the track. Alice immediately went for her rifle and waited to see what appeared. Suddenly a convoy of eight army trucks and two Humvee's pitched into view and Alice breathed a sigh of relief but still kept her rifle close by. The convoy drew to a halt and an officer stepped out of the passenger side of the 'Ranger Special Operations Vehicle' heading up the front. Alice's eyes kept flitting between the impressive looking jeep which had two machine guns installed, one pointing forwards and one pointing aft, and the officer who was making his way over to her with two guards who had fallen in behind him.

The officer looked Alice up and down: she was wearing camouflage trousers and jacket, and an army cap. The officer smiled and said, "Well, where did you spring from ma'am. We haven't seen anyone for twenty-four hours."

Alice looked the officer up and down; he was an impressive looking man: tall with grey hair and a slight paunch. It occurred to her that in his younger days he was probably quite handsome.

"We've been keeping to roads like these since yesterday, looking for somewhere to set up a base of operations," continued the general.

"I'm up here doing a recce, we have a base about an hour away from here," said Alice.

"Let me introduce myself," said the officer, extending his hand, "General Glenn Jackson, at your service."

"Alice Denham," replied Alice, then added, "sir."

"You're not military are you?" said General Jackson.

"In these desperate times don't you think we are all military?"

General Jackson nodded, it was a fair point. "You don't sound American," continued Jackson, "are you British?"

Alice thought about this for a few seconds and eventually said, "There aren't any nationalities – no countries anymore, just them and us, General – them and us."

"Amen to that," agreed Jackson solemnly.

"You said "we" earlier," he continued, "how many of you are there?"

"About twenty-five personnel – mostly National Guard – and a few vehicles. I was about to head back, perhaps you'd like to follow me?"

"That would be fine," said General Jackson, "lead the way."

The convoy followed Alice, and an hour later a loud rumble of trucks could be heard from inside the base. A number of troops went for their weapons and then relaxed as Alice's Range Rover drove into the clearing followed by the convoy.

Alice got out to see a very annoyed Joe staring at her.

"What the hell!" he exclaimed, "we'll talk about this later."

Before Alice could give him an answer Joe walked straight past her, made his way over to the jeep and introduced himself to General Jackson. Then they set about organising the vehicles and billeting down the troops. The clearing was a hive of activity as more tents and awnings were erected, becoming more and more like a military base.

"This is an excellent base to operate from, Sergeant," said Jackson. "You did well to organise it. Who is in charge here?"

"I can't really take the credit, sir," said Joe. "Alice and the two others in the RV have been here for some time now. I am the most senior officer here but the person you really need to speak to is Dr Middlebrook in the RV." Joe continued, "You got a plan, sir?"

"I've got an idea up my sleeve, we are desperately short of weapons and ammo, but that can wait," said Jackson thoughtfully. "Introduce me to the people in this RV – oh interesting girl that Alice, I like her."

Joe led General Jackson over to the RV where Middlebrook and Anna were watching. He introduced them and walked back into the centre of the base to assess their strength.

"You've got to do something about her, she's a fucking liability." It was Katlin who had just stormed up to him and was fuming. "She's going to get us all killed."

Holding his hands out to fend Katlin off, Joe said, "I know, I know, I'll have a word with her later."

"Just be sure you do," fumed Katlin still unable to contain herself, "or I will."

Katlin walked off and Joe glanced over at the RV, he knew that he was going to have to find a way to rein Alice in but he couldn't be too hard on her. After all she had, albeit more by luck than judgement, brought in much needed provisions, and brought the convoy back. Feeling relieved that the burden of leadership had now been lifted off his shoulders, Joe went to find something to eat.

CHAPTER EIGHT
D.U.M.B.

Two and a half hours of being jostled about in the back of the trucks, was beginning to take its toll, when suddenly the convoy finally turned left onto a track that led into deep woodland.

Sensing the turn Joe said, "It feels like we're off the main road."

A soldier at the rear of the truck looked out and confirmed this to be the case and as the track narrowed they could hear branches rubbing and scraping along the sides. Everyone started to get fidgety and apprehensive with anticipation, realising that they must be close now. A further twenty minutes went by until eventually the convoy ground to a halt.

General Jackson, riding at the front in his RSOV jeep, marshalled the troops and called for silence. He surveyed the area squinting in the darkness to make sense of the terrain. Eventually he found what he was looking for: a line of trees that looked too uniform to be natural. As he made his way through them he motioned for the rest of his men to follow. About fifty feet through the other side of the tree line, a pair of huge steel doors came into view, built into a rock face. Jackson walked straight up to a box to the side and slightly proud of the wall. He lifted a small flap to reveal a keypad and entered a six digit number. A panel automatically slid open. Then a piece of apparatus moved mechanically into position. Jackson wasted no time: he placed his right eye against the eyepiece and paused.

A few seconds later the apparatus responded with, "Retinal recognition confirmed – Access granted – Welcome General Jackson."

With that the hefty steel doors slowly swung inwards to reveal a massive ovoid tunnel that led deep into the ground at a slight slope.

Half of the company were left outside to stand guard whilst Jackson led the rest into the tunnel. As they moved forwards lights came on in front of them automatically to illuminate the way. Alice was astounded, how could such a massive construction exist and for no one to know anything about it. Jackson stopped to address his men,

"Okay, listen up. About two hundred yards down here on the left is a platform that will take us down several levels. Let's get to it quickly."

On reaching this point Jackson opened the door and twenty-five of the fifty men stepped in. Alice being one of them noticed that the floor levels indicated on the control panel went down to level twelve. Jackson pressed the button for level seven and the platform began to slowly descend. At level seven the platform stopped and everyone stepped out. Jackson led them to a large room. It was empty but for several trollies and another keypad on one wall. Putting in yet another code Jackson stepped back to allow the door to slide open and reveal what appeared to be another wall. At four feet from the ground on this second wall was a line of equally spaced wheels painted red.

Jackson called a soldier over, "Help me with this."

And as they turned the first wheel on the far right clockwise, a section of the wall four feet thick slid sideways to make a gap revealing rows and rows of guns of all shapes and sizes, plus boxes of ammunition on either side.

"Okay people, let's start getting these mothers loaded onto trollies and taken up to ground level." ordered Jackson.

One by one, each wheel was turned to slide another part of the wall across. Some soldiers were tasked with taking trollies up to the waiting truck that had reversed into the tunnel whilst the rest, including Joe and Alice, were left to load trollies. Alice and Joe turned one of the wheels and when the panel slid sideways they walked in with two other soldiers following behind. What they saw however was not guns or ammo but rows of olive green oversize backpacks.

"What the hell are these!" exclaimed Joe.

"My God," replied one of the soldiers, "they look like SADMs. I thought they were decommissioned years ago.

"SADMs?" enquired Alice none the wiser.

"Yeah, Special Atomic Demolition Munitions," continued the soldier, "though these look smaller and lighter than the old W54's."

"You mean these are nuclear bombs!" exclaimed Alice in disbelief.

"That's right, backpack nukes," the voice of General Jackson coming from behind surprised them, "about fifteen kiloton and a destruction radius of about half a mile. Leave them and let's get on."

They all left except Alice who hung back, then she went over to the backpacks, considered them for a minute and lifted one down. Alice picked it up by the wide, well-padded shoulder straps. It was heavy but light enough to be easily carried on one's back. She put two of the bombs onto a trolley and tried to get Joe's attention. Joe saw Alice beckoning him back into the room and walked over to her.

"Help me get these up top," hissed Alice in a hushed tone.

"Are you mad? We can't take these – they're nukes for God's sake."

"I don't care, better to have them than not." replied Alice insistently.

With that Alice started to wheel them into the lift with Joe helping reluctantly. They hid the bombs amongst the rest of the trollies and they were brought out into the tunnel to be loaded to the second truck. Nobody noticed as Joe lifted them in and placed them deep inside the truck so that they were less likely to be seen.

Joe waited for Alice to make an appearance and when she didn't show, decided to go back down to look for her when the platform made its next descent. He found her among the busy soldiers, delving into shelves looking for anything that might be of use. Seeing Joe walking over to her with an impatient look on his face, Alice, ignoring it, beckoned to him.

"What do you think might be in that case?"

Joe looked up to where Alice was pointing. On one of the higher shelves was a smooth metallic looking case.

"Who knows," replied Joe rhetorically, forgetting his annoyance, his interest piqued. "Let's get it down and check it out."

To get the case to the floor took some effort though it was more awkward than heavy. Joe released the catch, surprised that it wasn't locked. When they lifted the lid they were presented with what looked like six guns in a neat line, held in position by metal clips. They were however, nothing like what Joe had ever seen before, slightly larger than a pistol, the shiny silver weapons looked alien in design. Alice picked one up to examine more closely.

"It's a bit Dan Dare," she said with a chuckle, "where's the trigger?"

Joe was mystified too; he couldn't find a trigger either. A sudden realisation came over Alice. "These must be the weapons made from the plans that Karen, the time traveller I told you about, gave to Barny. They built these quick."

The weapon was futuristic looking for sure reflected Joe, he had no better explanation. Alice moved her hand to the grip and clasped it. Immediately the weapon sprang into life and metallic panels expanded from the guns rear and wrapped themselves around her wrist and part of the way up her forearm.

"Bloody hell – what's happening?" said Alice panicking.

"I don't know," replied Joe trying to prize the gun off her, "It's almost as if the thing's become a part of you."

Not wanting to be seen with the gun stuck to her right arm, they moved to an unoccupied area to try and figure it out without attracting attention.

"It's no good," said Joe exasperated, "it won't budge."

Studying it a little closer Alice said, "Do you think it's loaded?" Clearly there was power as displayed by the three small red lights glowing on the left hand side.

"If it is then how the hell do you fire it?"

Alice pointed the gun at the wall and to her astonishment a thin yellow laser shot out and burnt a small hole in the wall.

"How did you do that?" said an equally astonished Joe.

Alice shrugged and said, "I just thought *fire damn it* and it did."

"Are you trying to tell me this thing operates by thought?"

"I dunno," she replied, "hang on, let me try something." Alice lowered her right arm and thought *release*. Immediately the weapon unwrapped itself from her arm and shut down. "Yes – definitely by thought," said Alice triumphantly with a grin.

"Incredible!" exclaimed Joe, "let me have a go."

Alice passed the gun over to Joe who held it by the grip. Nothing happened.

"Why did it work for you and not me?"

Alice took the gun back and once again it attached itself to her and again she was able to release it.

"Try another one," said Alice.

Joe picked up another gun with his right hand and held the grip. Just like with Alice the weapon sprang into life and wrapped itself around his forearm.

"They must configure themselves to whoever picks them up first," said Joe in amazement, releasing it from his arm, "we'd better take these with us."

They put the case onto a trolley and took it up to the waiting truck. Soldiers were beginning to load boxes onto the third truck and Alice and Joe managed to get the shiny metal case loaded without arousing suspicion or awkward questions.

Being almost full, the truck was ordered to move forwards to allow one final truck to be loaded. It rolled out of the tunnel and stopped behind the tree line and as the fourth truck was starting to manoeuvre into position so that it could reverse down the tunnel, a yellow laser beam shot from somewhere in the darkness, hit the truck square on and it burst into flames. Hastily soldiers moved away. The heat was intense from the inferno which was lighting up the night sky. The driver opened the door and collapsed on the ground, his whole body aflame. He writhed for a few seconds and then lay still. Seconds later the truck exploded and men threw themselves to the ground for cover.

Startled, Joe and Alice, who were still in the tunnel, came running out to a hail of laser fire. Most of the soldiers were still on the ground trying to keep their heads from being blown off. Those brave enough to return fire, were hit by the constant stream of laser beams coming through the trees. Alice took her new weapon and held the grip almost immediately it was operational. Joe saw and just as he was about to do the same, he was hit by a laser beam. He fell to ground close to the loaded truck and Alice distraught, knelt beside him. She could see a deep gash in his scalp. Katlin who had been on sentry duty, saw what happened and came rushing over. She knelt over Joe to see how bad he was.

"Is he dead?" cried Alice.

Katlin put a finger to his neck to feel for a pulse. "No – he's alive – just. I can feel a faint pulse, We need to get him into the back of the truck."

Alice just froze there doing nothing.

"Come on Alice." urged Katlin.

Alice came to her senses and moved into action. "Get into the back of the truck," said Alice, "I'll try and lift him up to you."

"What's that," enquired Katlin nodding towards the new laser weapon which Alice had just placed on the ground.

"There's no time, I'll tell you about them later,"

With all the strength she could muster, Alice lifted the dead weight up to Katlin who put her hands under Joe's arms and helped to pull him in.

"Now you," shouted Katlin above the din, "we can't stay here."

"There's no room," shouted Alice shaking her head, "you go – I'll take one of the other trucks." With that Alice banged on the side of the truck for the driver to pull away then she watched as the truck disappeared down the track into the night.

When Alice carefully peaked through the tree line, she could see that there were five trucks still intact. Whilst they were manoeuvring out of the line of fire she noticed General Jackson and another soldier returning fire from the RSOV jeep's two machine guns. The trucks didn't get very far before a fireball a foot in diameter bolted through the air at great speed and hit one of the trucks, which lifted slightly in the air due to the force of the explosion. Alice recoiled at the intense heat then four more fireballs came through in quick succession destroying the other four trucks. The blaze was huge lighting up the night sky to the point where Alice could see soldiers scampering around trying to find cover. The tree line was starting to catch fire also so Alice moved around them to avoid the heat and falling branches. General Jackson and the soldier were still returning fire seemingly firing blindly in the general direction of the attack, when a fireball hit the jeep and sent it flying into the air in a ball of flames.

The jeep summersaulted and landed upside down in a flaming crumpled heap.

It wasn't looking good; her means of a quick getaway had had just been destroyed. The only option being to try and sneak out through the forest without being seen. As she made her move a salvo of fireballs hit the mountain around the entrance to the underground base and large chunks of rock and stone dropped, blocking off and filling up the gap. Soldiers who were taking shelter from the laser fire were entombed with no hope of rescue.

Alice carefully and as silently as possible picked her way from tree to tree, paused behind one tree and heard a noise coming in her direction. She peeked round it: a Deviant was walking towards her. She stepped out and shot him full in the chest with her laser gun. The Deviant dropped to the ground – killed instantly. Alice walked up to him and saw that he was wearing what looked like goggles. Removing them, Alice put the goggles to her face. They were for night vision and suddenly she could see what was happening around her. Deviants were making a sweep through the forest picking off any soldier they came across. A laser beam shot past close to her left shoulder and she jumped behind a tree. Working her way around the tree she saw her assailant and shot at him. This time she hit his left shoulder, he reeled backwards, but before he hit the ground Alice gave off another burst and killed him. It was difficult to ascertain which way to go, every direction seemed to take her deeper into the hornet's nest. She moved to another tree which seemed to give better cover and paused to decide her next move. From behind a hand clasped her mouth, preventing her from making a sound. The figure moved round in front of her and put his finger to his mouth to indicate silence, he was too big and muscular to be a Black Eye.

"Cardenas," she hissed in a hushed tone, "you scared the crap out of me."

"Sorry," he grinned, "I've been watching you; I didn't want you shooting me."

"I took these night vision goggles from a dead Black Eye."

"Yes I know," he replied. Cardenas tried them on and nodded his approval.

"How bad is it?" continued Alice.

"Those bastards are killing everyone. It's slaughter out there."

"What about Sherman?" enquired Alice, "have you seen him?"

"Listen, hear that pounding sound over there?"

Cardenas pointed in the general direction of the slow but steady boom-boom of Sherman's M2 machine gun. Alice had heard it earlier but was too busy to perceive its significance. They paused and listened for a few minutes to try and ascertain how far away he was.

Two hundred yards to their left, Sherman was struggling with overwhelming odds. He was spraying 0.50 calibre shells and Nih-troopers were dropping like skittles then suddenly his machine gun jammed. Sherman tried to unjam the gun but it was no good. He threw it to the ground and pulled out his Bowie knife. It was a defiant but ultimately futile gesture. A laser beam hit him on the left knee and shattered the joint. Grimacing in pain, Sherman started to keel over sideways until another shot hit him in the right knee and he slumped down kneeling in the mud.

The Nih-troopers approached him and one picked up the knife he had just dropped. It was Mida who moved closer holding the knife in front of a dazed Sherman swaying unsteadily on his knees.

"You put up a brave fight, but your luck has just run out," said Mida dispassionately. With that she walked behind him pulled back his head and slit his throat. Blood spurted out of Sherman's neck and ran down his front. Mida gave him a shove and he fell forwards on his face into a puddle, then wiping the blade clean on Sherman's back, she inspected the knife closer. "Nice blade – I think I shall keep it."

Whilst removing the sheath from Sherman's belt, Mida and the Nih-troopers' attention was jolted by machine gun fire over on their far right.

"Binoculars," demanded Mida of a trooper.

Mida took the binoculars and looked in the direction of the noise. With night vision she could make out a large man shooting from behind a tree. She continued to scan around until she stopped on another tree. Mida could just about make out part of another figure hiding behind the tree. She switched the binoculars to scanner mode which made the tree look translucent. The figure behind became clear and Mida gave a gasp of delight.

"Well, well, Alice Denham," she said to herself, "serendipity indeed."

She rallied her troops and led them around away from the gunfire in an attempt to sneak up on Alice.

The machine gun fire stopped abruptly, Sherman was either dead or out of ammunition, which would ultimately amount to the same thing. Cardenas and Alice looked at each other and said nothing. They both knew what the silence meant.

"We need to keep moving or we'll become sitting ducks."

Alice nodded her agreement and very carefully they started to move forwards, with Alice in front using the night vision goggles to pick out their way. More Deviants came into view and Alice shot at them before they could react. Cardenas was impressed at the way she was prepared to shoot without hesitation and joined her in the fire fight with his semi-automatic. Alice crept past several more trees, one by one, when suddenly she was pinned to a tree by four red belts which shot through the air, wrapped around her body and legs, and around the back of a tree trunk. Her head hit the trunk of the tree with force and momentarily she lost consciousness. The laser gun automatically dropped from her arm and hit the ground. Cardenas approached the tree from behind and took out his knife.

"Alice I'm going to try and get you free."

Lifting her head Alice gave a slight groan and tried to shake herself to her senses. Putting his hand under her chin Cardenas said, "Alice, are you with me?"

"Yes – forget me – save yourself."

Cardenas ignored her, placed his knife on the top strap and tried to cut through. "What's this stuff made of?" he said frantically, "my knife won't touch it."

Alice heard a thump beside her; it was Cardenas hitting the ground. He had been shot in the temple and twice in the chest. He was killed instantly. Watching through the night vision goggles, Alice could see a group of Deviants approaching her. One came up close and ripped the goggles off her head knowing that she must have killed one of their own to obtain them.

Another Deviant came closer and Alice recognised her instantly. It was the female from her dream.

Smiling, the Deviant said, "Alice Denham. So this is where you bolted to. We've been looking for you. HT Mida Raar," she continued, bowing in mock humility.

"The pleasure is all yours I'm sure." snarled Alice frightened but determined to remain defiant.

Mida stepped closer. "I watched you all those months ago through your wall – seems you've grown a backbone at last." Mida took Sherman's Bowie knife and held it against Alice's throat. "Shall I let you live?" she said playfully, "or shall I carve you up?"

Alice recognised the knife, it was the one used by Mida in her dream.

"My God you're an ugly troll." said Alice, refusing to be intimidated and attempting to get the upper hand in the conversation.

Mida stuck out her forked tongue and hissed in anger then she slapped Alice hard across the face with the back of her hand. Alice's head was knocked sideways from the impact and she felt a sting of pain. Licking her split lower lip Alice felt the blood which was now oozing from the cut. She decided it was prudent not to provoke Mida further and fell silent.

"Choose you words carefully my dear," said Mida gripping Alice's chin tightly, "believe me, I'm your worst nightmare."

Alice whipped her head to one side forcing Mida to release her grip.

"Release her and bring her with me." commanded Mida.

Alice was released from the tree and man handled away by a Nih-trooper.

Mida intervened, "I don't want her harmed, is that clear?"

The trooper nodded and took her away. Alice gave one last look over her shoulder at Cardenas lying by the tree. All that could be heard in the forest was the crackle of flames reaching high into the night sky, signifying that the fight was over. Two Nih-troopers grabbed Alice's arms and dragged her off towards the transport that would take her back to their base, and as they disappeared into the night an eerie silence fell over the forest.

* * *

It was gone 1.00am when the first truck rolled into camp. Middlebrook had stayed up all night, too anxious about the mission to sleep. Anna appeared at the door of the RV, woken from her restless slumber by the noise of the truck.

Middlebrook approached the driver as he was getting out of the cabin.

"Where's the rest?"

"There should be more along soon," replied the driver, "we left as soon as we loaded up."

Sure enough the second truck appeared about thirty minutes later. Finally, the third truck rolled in but this time Middlebrook could see by the beleaguered expression on the driver's face that something was wrong. Katlin jumped down from the back and clearly distressed, approached Middlebrook.

"It just came out of nowhere," she cried, "we were ambushed – laser fire everywhere. They got Joe – he's in the back here unconscious."

"What about the rest?" replied Middlebrook. "Where's Alice?"

"Gone," said Katlin. "I saw the rest of the trucks blow up as we were leaving. And the General's jeep's gone."

"The General's dead?"

Katlin just nodded and said, "Alice helped me get Joe onto this truck. I tried to get to her come with us but she insisted on taking one of the other trucks."

"We need to get Joe comfortable," continued Katlin, "where can we put him?"

Middlebrook turned to the driver who was standing nearby staring into the distance seemingly in a daze. "Did you bring ay stretchers with you?"

The driver didn't respond at first and Middlebrook had to shake him out of his malaise. He pointed to a tent and walked away then Katlin ran off to get the stretcher.

"We'll put him in Alice's bed," said Anna, "he will be more comfortable there."

Katlin returned and as they loaded Joe onto the stretcher he could see, even in the dark, the extent of Joe's injury. Middlebrook looked at Anna doubtfully – it didn't look good.

With Joe tucked up in Alice's bed in the RV, Middlebrook was able to inspect the wound more closely. His skull had been burnt away in a line about two inches long and half an inch wide, but what really concerned Middlebrook was the fact that his brain had been exposed.

"It looks like there might be some brain damage," said Middlebrook gravely, "We won't know for sure until he regains consciousness; if he does at all."

Katlin sat on the edge of the bed and took Joe's hand in hers, looking at him forlornly.

"You know I've loved him ever since we first met over ten years ago," she said with tears running down her cheeks. "We go back a long way me and Joe."

Anna and Middlebrook stood there and listened.

"He was engaged to his wife at the time," she continued through her sobs, "and when she passed away I thought there might be hope for us – you know when he was ready."

Katlin's voice changed to a slightly harsher tone. "Then Alice turned up and ruined everything."

Anna and Middlebrook looked at each other; they had no idea and didn't know how to respond.

"I don't know for sure what happened to Alice, the last time I saw her she was running into the trees," said Katlin looking up at Middlebrook, "there's a part of me that hopes that she is dead. Does that make me a bad person?"

"No – you're not a bad person," reassured Middlebrook putting a comforting arm around her shoulder, "that's just human nature."

A gun shot rang out on the other side of the base, startling all three who immediately stepped out of the RV to see what was happening. Two other soldiers carrying rifles were running to the tent where the gun shot came from.

By the time Middlebrook, Anna and Katlin got to the tent the two soldiers were standing at the entrance staring in. Middlebrook had the presence of mind to pick up a torch and switched it on as he entered the tent. The driver of Katlin's truck was sprawled across his bunk with a rifle lying across his chest.

Middlebrook scanned the beam around. A spray of blood was dripping down the inside of the tent with pieces of brain and bone sliding down the canvas.

Walking up to the dead soldier, Middlebrook noticed a piece of paper in his hand. Prying it from the man's fingers he opened it up and saw just three words – he read it out loud.

"There's no hope."

Middlebrook screwed up the note and walked out of the tent and breathed in deeply. Anna put her arm around him seeing that he was shocked.

Middlebrook shook himself to his senses and said, "Wrap him up; we'll deal with it later. It's late and we should all try and get some sleep."

Before walking to her tent Katlin said, "Don't let him die Doc, there's been enough death today."

Middlebrook didn't reply as he watched her walk away. How could he possibly promise her anything? He wasn't a medical doctor and their medical supplies were virtually non-existent.

Very soon Anna and Middlebrook were lying in bed. Anna moved close to cuddle up.

"There's something that you should know," said Anna apprehensively. "I think Alice might be pregnant."

"What!" exclaimed a startled Middlebrook sitting up in bed, "how long have you known?"

"She told me this morning that she is two days late and normally she is regular as clockwork."

"Why didn't you tell me?"

"She swore me to secrecy. She knew you wouldn't allow her to go on the mission if you knew. You know what she's like. And besides we can't be certain at this point if she has conceived, it's too early to tell."

"Did Joe know?" said Middlebrook calming down a little and realising that he was talking about Joe in the past tense.

"No I don't think so," replied Anna, "I'm sure he would have stopped her too."

Middlebrook sat there thinking for a moment. "My God! – It's this baby that Karen must have meant in my office back at St. Clare's last year, not the one that miscarried."

"There's a good chance Alice is still alive," he continued, "this baby might just be her salvation."

"That's not all," said Anna, "I'm pregnant as well."

Middlebrook was stunned into silence, his mind racing. "How long have you known?" he said eventually.

"Just a few days," she replied, "I've been waiting for the right time to tell you. We must have conceived fairly closely to each other."

Middlebrook held Anna close, sensing that she needed reassurance. He had to admit however, it was a hell of world to bring a baby into.

Anna drifted off to sleep in his arms and soon he could hear her gentle breathing. Still running the implications of Alice's possible pregnancy through his mind, Middlebrook tried to get some sleep too. Tomorrow was going to be a busy day.

CHAPTER NINE
THE LAST PATROL

Dawn was just about to break as Alice and Katlin looked from their vantage point high on the mountain ledge. The sun had not yet risen above the horizon though the sky was showing signs of getting lighter. Intermittent cloud cover had a salmon pink hue and as they looked to the valley below, the wispy white flurries of mist were already starting to burn off. Alice and Katlin looked at each other and smiled, then they held hands and turned to look again at the sun which was now starting to show itself. The sky burst with a bright yellow wash of light and Alice and Katlin hugged each other tightly. As they did so, they gradually started turning to rock, until eventually it was impossible to discern one from the other. They had become part of the mountain, an obelisk pointing to the sky, high on the rocky outcrop. Then a strong wind began to blow and started to erode the obelisk. Starting at the top, dust flew away, with the wind wearing it down until no trace could be seen. Just as the last flurries of dust were about to be blown away, Alice woke up with a start. *What the hell was that about*, she thought.

Alice rubbed her face and tried to focus on her surroundings. Her head was pounding, partly from hitting the back of her head on the tree trunk and also from the strong sedation administered by her captors. Thirsty and with an unpleasant taste in her mouth, Alice looked around to see she was in a plain grey room with no furnishings other than the bed she was now sitting on, then she became aware of the fact that she was also wearing a white hospital type gown instead of her uniform. In front of her was a wall with a gap to one side. Standing up, Alice walked unsteadily to see what was behind it. Leaning on the edge of the wall she looked in to see a toilet, sink and shower cubicle. Walking back to her bed, Alice sat down and wondered how long she had been unconscious. Then a hatch opened in another wall and a shelf protruded. On it was a glass of water, a small dish with a pill in it, what looked like a bowl of cereal, and her army uniform freshly laundered. A voice seemed to come out of nowhere and made Alice jump.

"Medication, for your head. Please, refresh and replenish," said the monotone voice.

Alice took the pill, reasoning that if they were going to kill her they would have done it by now. After eating the food she decided to have a shower. Everything that she needed was in the en suite: gel, shampoo, and towels. The pill was starting to take effect and Alice stepped into the shower enjoying the comfortably warm water that was flowing over her body.

While Alice showered completely unaware, Drypha and Mida watched down on her through a one-way viewing gallery with the dispassionate interest of a primatologist studying a chimpanzee. Mida studied her, unimpressed.

"We have better specimens." she said.

"True," concurred Drypha, "she's acceptable enough though it's not her body that we're interested in. Alice has displayed interesting psychic abilities – and she is pregnant."

"Pregnant! I didn't know."

"Make sure she is kept comfortable," Drypha continued, "tomorrow she will be taken to the laboratory."

* * *

Alice was woken up on the second day by a door opening to her cell. She had no idea how long she had been asleep or whether it was day or night. Three Deviants entered wearing light blue gowns and wheeling a stretcher trolley.

"What's this for? Where are you taking me?" she cried in alarm.

The technicians said nothing but tried to persuade a protesting Alice to lie down on the trolley. Eventually they had to sedate her to gain her to cooperation. Alice was in a semi-conscious state vaguely aware that she was travelling down a narrow corridor which ultimately opened up into what looked like a high-tech operating theatre. Alice was lifted from the trolley and placed on a table tilted slightly forwards. Metal straps automatically arced across to restrain her: one across her neck, one across each wrist and one across each ankle. As she became conscious again, Alice realised that she was completely immobile. The strap around her neck, though not strangling her, was tight enough to prevent her lifting her head.

"She's coming round," said one of the technicians, "we will have to sedate her properly before we can start."

A mask was placed over Alice's nose and mouth and soon she fell into a deep sleep.

It could have been hours, days or even weeks when Alice woke up to see tubes protruding from her abdomen and several sensor pads attached to her arms and chest. She didn't have time to react however, before the apparatus automatically sensed her conscious state and put her back under again.

This became Alice's routine deep sleep interspersed with moments of semi-consciousness, vaguely aware of people looking over her and walking away to adjust apparatus. Days drifted into weeks and weeks drifted into months until eventually nine months later Alice was back in her cell as if nothing had happened.

Alice slid her legs off the side of the bed and tried to stand up. She grimaced a little and held her abdomen. Lifting the gown that she was wearing to find a horizontal scar six inches long about five inches below her naval.

"My God," she cried out in panic, realising that they had performed a caesarean section on her, "what have you done to me? Where is my baby?"

She had no idea at what point in the pregnancy the baby had been removed. Alice sat back down on the bed, her face in her hands, she said through her tears, "Where's my baby?"

Then she grew angry, stood up, walked over to a wall and banged it with all her might with the sides of her fists. "Let me out of here you bastards," she screamed, "or..." Her voice trailed off, *or what?* she thought.

The monotone voice responded, "Are you not comfortable?"

"It's a prison," she replied with all the contempt that she could muster, "it doesn't matter how comfortable it is, it's still a prison. What have you done with my baby?"

"You went full term," continued the voice, "and gave birth to a healthy child. The infant is safe."

"Nine months, I've been away that long," she retorted, "can I see it – please let me see it."

Alice realised that she did not know the sex of the child. "Is it a boy or a girl?"

The voice remained silent and Alice eventually slumped onto the bed and sobbed into her pillow.

* * *

Sitting upright on the bed with her knees brought up to her chest, Alice contemplated the folly and the ramifications of her actions. She was so wrapped up in taking revenge on what the Black Eyes had done to her life that she didn't stop to think of the implications it might have for her baby. And now she was paying the price. Alice sat there for an indeterminate length of time wondering what would become of her, she had no clock or window from which to gauge the passing of the day or indeed days. She exercised, ate when food appeared through the hatch, and slept when she felt tired. No one came to the room and the monotone voice that irritated her so much remained taciturn.

Then one evening outside her cell, the control panel that gained access, started to light up. A bleep sounded and the door clicked open a few inches, rousing Alice from her doze. She looked at the door expectantly but nobody entered, so walking over to it she gingerly put her head out into the corridor to take a peek. Puzzled, Alice walked back and sat on the end of her bed.

What is this? she thought, *some kind of trick*?

After several minutes of listening intently and hearing no activity outside of the cell, Alice hurriedly dressed into her army uniform. As she finished putting her boots on, she heard a voice in her head, Go – *quickly.*

Alice put a hand to her head, did she really hear that? Then the voice came again but more insistent this time: Go – *now.*

Once again Alice hesitantly poked her head outside the door. The corridor was empty but which direction should she take? Left or right? *Left*, said the voice in her head.

Alice stepped into the corridor, pulled the door shut as quietly as possible and made her way down the corridor. Several minutes later after a hurried walk, she came to a staircase to the left hand side. Since the mysterious voice seemed to be helping her, Alice paused for more guidance. Much to her annoyance nothing happened so acting instinctively, Alice climbed the staircase. At the top she opened the door which gave way to a small semi-circular room with three doors equally spaced on the curved wall opposite. Sighing with exasperation, Alice had no idea which door to choose, so she walked past them all and thought to hell with it and opened the middle door, then made her way down yet another long corridor. Eventually she could see an end in front of her and Alice became aware of side corridors to the left and right. Alice stopped at each side corridor to ensure no one was there to apprehend her before moving on. The corridors were deserted so she made her way carefully to the opening.

What she saw however amazed her.

The corridor opened out onto a gangway which looked down onto a wide apron for vehicles of all shapes and sizes to set down on. Lights of all colours were flashing intermittently, some guiding vessels to land. There was a constant furore of activity as the shiny golden vessels parked up. Alice's attention was drawn to the far end of the apron, where floating just above the ground was one of the half orbs. It looked massive and as she watched transfixed two vessels flew into it and disappeared. Then one vessel came out. Realising that the orb was a time portal for this particular outpost and being at the centre of operations, she was in danger of being detected. Backtracking slightly, Alice took a side corridor to the right and as she made her way down, she could hear the sound of people approaching at the far end. They were out of sight but Alice knew that she had to do something and quick. Desperately looking around for somewhere to hide Alice could see nowhere and then she looked up. Above her was a vent opening about three feet square without a grille. Also to her astonishment there was a ladder in the vent which could be pulled down to gain access. The ceiling wasn't high and as she reached up her finger tips were about six inches from the first rung. Alice jumped, her fingers touched the first rung but she couldn't get a grip. She jumped again with more force this time and got a hold on the ladder which slid down onto the floor. Without hesitation Alice climbed the ladder into the vent and pulled it up behind her. Just in time, as a small group of Nih-troopers turned a corner into the corridor where Alice had just been standing. She watched them pass beneath her and waited until they were out of earshot before she started to make a move. The vent was uncomfortably warm but she knew this was probably her best means of escape without being discovered.

The venting system was a labyrinth of tunnels and Alice navigated her way randomly until eventually she was hit by a gentle breeze of cooler air. As quietly as she could Alice made her way towards the cool air and very soon she was staring down a vertical circular shaft that dropped about fifty feet. The shaft was barely two feet in diameter but the sides were ribbed so Alice decided to try and make her way down. Easing herself in she worked her way down until eventually the shaft turned horizontal. Alice had no choice but crawl backwards on her hands and knees until very soon she came to an obstruction. The cool breeze was stronger and fresher now and looking behind her as best as she could, Alice could see a grille and the dark of night outside. Crawling backwards up to the grille, she started kicking and after several attempts it began to shift. Eventually the grille dropped away and Alice was hanging from the opening for a short drop to the ground. She was free.

With no one in the near vicinity, she made her way quickly across a clearing and into the woods beyond. A fast flowing river could be heard in the background and its turbulent roar slowly abated as Alice made her way deeper into the forest. After walking for more than an hour or so she stopped to catch her breath. Looking back the way she had come, there was no sign of the Deviant outpost nor was anyone following her, though she realised that her escape would be detected by morning, she must get as many miles under her belt as possible. With that, Alice disappeared into the pitch black interior of the forest.

By morning the alarm was raised when Alice's absence became apparent. Drypha was in the laboratory watching a female human worker fussing over Alice's baby. It was

Karen Foster who had managed to survive her trip back despite not accomplishing her mission. A nervous guard approached Drypha to give him the bad news.

"The human – Alice, is not in her cell, sir."

"How did she get out!" exclaimed Drypha. The guard shrugged nervously, he had no idea. Mida came rushing in and walked straight up to Drypha.

"Have you heard?"

Drypha nodded but seemed unperturbed.

"We've searched the whole complex. She seems to have just disappeared. Someone must have helped the bitch," insisted Mida looking over at Karen.

"It wasn't her," said Drypha, "she doesn't have the security clearance." "It's of no consequence," he continued looking over at the baby in Karen's arms, "it's a shame we can't run more tests on the girl, but we have what we want, so let her go. After all what harm can she do us."

* * *

Alice had no way of knowing exactly what the date was and could only guess that it must be late February, early March of the following year. In the small hours of the morning, making her way through the forest it certainly felt like winter or at the very least early spring. To keep warm Alice carried on walking through the night, jumping at every sound in the dense woodland.

By morning she had come out into open ground and was able to survey the terrain around her. She looked up at the sky to see mainly overcast cloud cover with intermittent breaks. It also became apparent that she was nowhere near where she was captured. Sitting down on a rock Alice looked at the grasslands ahead of her.

With no idea where she was, Alice realised that there was very little hope of getting back to Idaho and the relative safety of the base where Barny, Anna and Joe should be. Thoughts of Joe ran through her mind, did he survive his injury? She preferred to think that he did. Then it occurred to her that they may have moved on, especially if their position had been compromised. It suddenly dawned on Alice that her situation though not desperate wasn't good. She was cold, hungry and more importantly, had no water. With the early sun shining through a break in the clouds Alice had a good idea which way was east and decided to head in a westerly direction. After sitting still for a while Alice stood up to carry on. She wasn't used to hiking such distances and had stiffened up. Grimacing, she started walking west through the grassland. Feeling very exposed Alice was keen to get into cover again as soon as possible, and after several hours of trudging through the long grass she finally entered some woodland.

The overcast day made the forest gloomy and after a short distance in, Alice stopped in her tracks. About a hundred feet ahead of her was an old rundown wooden shack. Tentatively she crept up to the shack – there were no obvious signs of life so she tried to peer through a window to the side. The window was filthy and difficult to see through so Alice decided to try the door. Wincing at the creaking sound the door made as she opened it, Alice peered in and then slammed the door shut again. There was someone in there. Nothing happened and with her heart pounding, she opened the door and looked in again. Inside, the shack was rundown and dilapidated, with a table, two chairs and a cabinet against one wall. Sitting motionless in one of the chairs was an old man, his eyes were closed and Alice guessed that he must have been at least seventy years old. On closer scrutiny it was obvious he couldn't have been dead no more than a week. His skin was drained of colour and his lips were blue. Moving closer Alice looked for any kind of injury or disease but found nothing, deducing that he probably died of a heart attack or maybe just old age. What was certain however was that the corpse was beginning to smell and Alice had to cover her nose with her shirt. If the shack was going to be used Alice knew that she was going to have to get the body outside, so after wedging the door open she dragged the old man out to the nearest tree. Then she went back into the cabin and looked around for anything of use. The smell was still there but not so strong so she opened the only window to try and get rid of it. Hanging up on a nail was a red plaid lumberjack style coat with white fleece lining and white fleece collar. Alice inspected it and gave it a sniff. The coat was in good condition and smelt fine so Alice put it on. Ten minutes later she had found a canteen almost full of water. Some matches and two packs of beef jerky. In a corner she found a shovel and to ease her guilty conscience for robbing the poor old man, Alice decided to bury him. It was afternoon by the time she had finished the shallow grave and after placing a crude cross made of two sticks lashed together with a piece of string, Alice hot from her labours, thirsty and hungry sat down against the shack wall, ate some of the jerky and drank about half of the water in the canteen. Having gone without sleep for over twenty-four hours, Alice decided to stay here for the night and recharge her batteries. By the time darkness fell, and despite the fact that there was nowhere comfortable to lie down, Alice fell into a deep dreamless sleep, thoroughly exhausted.

The next morning she awoke to shafts of light piecing through gaps in the old shacks walls. Still aching from yesterday's excursions she did a few light exercises to loosen her limbs, picked up the canteen, jerky and matches, then left the cabin to carry on her journey. As she did so Alice lifted her cap to the grave as a mark of respect to the old man who unwittingly had helped her out.

For two days Alice ploughed on, sleeping rough at night and walking by day. Her food and water was now gone and she was beginning to feel very dehydrated. The forest had thinned out and given way to rocky outcrops and grass. To her right a mountain range loomed in the far distance. Sitting down on a rock, Alice decided to scan the area and make a decision where to go next. As she scanned, her attention was suddenly drawn to some movement in the distance. It looked like a small group of people picking their way slowly through the rocky terrain. Alice decided to try and catch up with them. Walking faster than she had been, Alice finally got close to the group about half an hour later. She was behind them now and when she got close enough, Alice called out. There were two adults and two children and they all turned around in alarm. The man brought his rifle to bear as Alice got closer.

"Don't come any closer ma'am," he shouted, pointing his gun in her direction.

"I haven't any weapons," replied Alice, "I mean you no harm."

Still suspicious the man motioned with his rifle for Alice to come closer while his family looked on nervously. When Alice got closer the man could see that Alice was not a threat and relaxed a little.

"You're the first people that I've seen in months," commented Alice.

"Where you headed?" the man said in a southern accent.

"I don't know, I've been walking aimlessly for days now and I'm hungry and thirsty."

"Well we ain't got nothing," said the man.

"Wade, we can spare a little," said his wife.

The woman approached and said to Alice, "We were about to stop and rest anyways." She led Alice over to the children and they all sat down. Wade put his rifle down and joined them.

"My name's Alice Denham."

She held out her hand to Wade who shook it.

My name's Wade and this is my wife Evelyn," he said, "and these two are Sophie and Darren."

Alice shook Evelyn's hand and smiled kindly at the children who looked about ten years old. The family looked malnourished and dishevelled, the children in particular resembled street urchins.

"I don't want to deprive you of anything," said Alice. "It's just nice to talk to someone."

"We can spare you a little," said Evelyn digging into her rucksack.

After eating a small piece of dry bread and cheese, Alice was keen for any news.

"I was captured by the Black Eyes over nine months ago but managed to escape a few days ago," she said, "can you tell me what's been happening?"

"Well," replied Wade giving the question some thought, "after those evil bastards showed, they started rounding up as many young girls as they could."

"How young?"

"Oh about eighteen to twenty-five," replied Evelyn, "thousands of them."

"Thousands? Why?"

Wade shrugged, "Didn't get a chance to ask them."

"Then after that," he continued, "these machines appeared – huge grey machines. They would position themselves in a circle on the outskirts of towns and cities and move inwards demolishing and destroying everything in their way. Nothing was left behind them but dust. When they reached the centre, they would join up to form a round object and take off to find another town to destroy. This country has virtually been levelled. Maybe the whole planet I guess."

"My God," was all that Alice could muster in reply. The situation was clearly hopeless. She looked at the family who were now looking down all forlorn. Then she looked out over the landscape and said as much to herself than anyone, "The battle is lost then."

"There are some small groups of folk still holding out," said Wade.

"Do you know where any of them might be?" asked Alice.

Pointing in a more southerly direction Wade said, "The last military encampment we heard of was some distance that way; maybe two hundred miles."

"Did you see them?" enquired Alice hopefully.

Wade shook his head, "Nope, just heard about them is all."

"Where are you heading for?"

Evelyn looked at Wade who replied, "Any place where we can settle and be safe. How about you Miss?"

"Well that direction is as good as any," stated Alice getting to her feet and pointing south.

Evelyn took hold of Alice's canteen and said, "Let me put some water in this for you."

"No, I couldn't possibly," protested Alice.

"It's okay," reassured Evelyn, "we can spare a little."

"Thank you," replied Alice, "thank you for everything."

"God's speed," said Evelyn, taking Alice's hand in hers.

Alice smiled back and nodded, then as they moved away, she waved them goodbye. Moving now in the direction in which Wade had pointed, Alice felt that she had at last a sense of purpose.

For two days she traversed the rocky landscape and by the time she encountered woodland again she was desperately hungry and out of water. With no option but to keep moving on in the hope that she might come across a stream, after two more days and nights, Alice was still in the forest and starting to feel faint from hunger and dehydration. Each morning she would wake up and the effort needed to carry on was becoming harder and harder to summon up. Eventually the forest started to thin out but Alice was staggering now, unable to focus properly – she was dizzy and disorientated. The trees seemed to be swaying as Alice looked up, or was it her, she could no longer tell. Alice steadied herself against a tree and thought that she glimpsed an open area ahead. Stumbling up to a track that ran along the edge of the forest Alice tripped over a large stone. Falling flat on her front she lay there unconscious, her upper body on the road, the rest of her concealed in long grass.

* * *

Katlin knew that this would be their last reconnaissance due to the shortage of fuel and was determined to make the most of it. She had taken the Humvee out with Corporal Ed Mitchell, one of the few remaining soldiers of General Jackson's company.

Ed was a tall, slim cautious man in his late twenties. He agreed reluctantly to take Katlin out on this patrol just to shut her up. Katlin had been bored and needed to feel that she was doing something positive.

"We'll have to turn back soon," stated Ed looking at the fuel gauge.

"I know Ed – just a little long eh?" replied Katlin.

"Okay, but stop calling me Ed, for pity's sake. Don't forget I outrank you, Private Grody."

"I'll start calling you Corporal when we start functioning as an operational unit and not pissing around camp doing nothing, going nowhere."

"Oh right," replied Ed rattled at Katlin's continual disrespect, "and with what? There's only a handful of us left."

"Just drive up to that ridge," said Katlin bored with the conversation, "we'll get a better view of the valley."

Ed drove the Humvee the short distance to the ridge and stopped. Katlin picked up her binoculars and stood on her seat. Poking her head through the opening in the roof, she could see a wide panoramic view of the valley below. The view was mostly woodland with a few open areas. In the far distance was a mountain range. She put the binoculars to her eyes and started to scan the area methodically. As she worked her way closer she noticed a track running along the edge of the forest. Katlin worked her binoculars up the track and then stopped and backed up a little. She could see something on the track, something red.

"Take a look at this," she said and then sarcastically added, "Corporal Mitchell, sir."

"What is it?" Ed ignored her tone and joined her through the roof.

"Not sure," said Katlin, "take a look."

She pointed in the general direction and handed the binoculars over to Ed who studied the mysterious object for few seconds.

"It looks like a body to me," he said, "about a mile away."

"Let me see again," Katlin looked and then said, "come on let's check it out."

"Wait – what if it's a trap."

"Really?" said Katlin incredulously. "When was the last time you saw any Black Eye activity. It's been months."

Reluctantly Ed started up the Humvee and reversed up and soon they were heading down the track to where the object was seen. It didn't take them long to reach the red object and Ed stopped twenty feet short. It was obvious now that it was in fact a body.

"Stay here, I'll take a look."

Ed got out and slowly walked up to the body, constantly looking around as if he expected something to come jumping suddenly out of the trees. He looked over the body and turned to Katlin.

"It's a girl," he shouted.

"Is she dead?"

Ed put his boot under her left shoulder and lifted it a few inches and then let it drop. There was no reaction from the girl.

"Yeah it looks like it."

Ed suddenly heard a growl coming from inside the tree line and could just make out a pack of dogs, of various breeds standing there, watching him. They were domestic dogs that had gone feral, and they were hungry.

"Private, you'd better get out here," said Ed nervously, "and bring your rifle."

Katlin didn't hear the growl but knew it must be serious; Ed never addressed her as Private. She quickly got out of the Humvee and approached.

"What is it?"

"Dogs, a whole pack of them."

The dogs were getting more aggressive, snarling and baring their teeth.

Katlin looked down at the girl in the red plaid lumberjack coat and her mouth opened in shock as recognition dawned on her. It was Alice. Her hair was longer but it was definitely her.

Getting bolder now, the dogs inched slowly closer.

"For God's sake what are you doing," cried an alarmed Ed, "shoot them."

Katlin snapped out of her reverie and sprayed a short burst at the pack. Three of the dogs were hit and killed outright and a further two were injured. The rest of the pack dispersed back into the woods. Katlin walked up to the injured dogs and put them out of their misery with a single shot each. She looked back at Alice still lying there inert. How could she possibly come back to haunt her alive or dead, especially after all this time, and where in God's name did she come from?

"I've had enough, let's get outta here," shouted Ed.

Katlin nodded and started to make her way back to the Humvee.

"Are you sure she's dead?" asked Katlin as they sat down and buckled up.

"Yes," replied Ed starting up the engine.

In the past Katlin had had dark thoughts about Alice, but seeing her like that she felt different. It didn't seem right somehow; just leaving her for dead.

Ed put the Humvee into gear and turned around to go back the way that they had come, then as he was about to pull away.

"Stop," shouted Katlin, "you didn't check her pulse. We must be certain."

Ed rolled his eyes and stopped. Katlin jumped out and ran back to Alice, then knelt beside her and put two fingers to the side of her neck. She felt nothing initially and was about to give up and then it happened – Katlin felt a very faint pulse.

"Back up closer," Katlin shouted, "she's alive."

"God dammit she's alive," she said to herself.

An astonished Ed reversed the Humvee and helped to load Alice into the back. Soon they were on their way back to camp. Katlin stayed silent for most of the journey with all manner of mixed emotions running through her head.

Boy have I got a surprise for Anna and the Doc, she thought.

* * *

Stepping out of his wooden shack late in the afternoon, Middlebrook looked around the settlement the surviving group had made for themselves. There were half a dozen wooden huts on one side and what to him looked like a smallholding. Various animals had been rescued from sorties out in the trucks and as a consequence they had a small flock of sheep, some goats, a pen full of chickens and even a couple of pigs. The other side of the settlement was taken up with attempts to grow vegetables. Their early endeavours had proven to be disastrous but they were getting better at it.

Middlebrook was worried; he had expected Katlin and Ed to be back two hours ago and there was still no sign of them. He was about to walk back into his hut when he heard the familiar rumble of the Humvee rolling into the camp.

Katlin got out first and ran over to Middlebrook.

"Where the hell have you been," said Middlebrook, "we've been worried sick."

"Never mind that Doc," she replied excitedly. "Come and see what we have got in the back." Katlin dragged a curious Middlebrook round to the back of the Humvee and opened up the door.

"Alice!" exclaimed Middlebrook, "where did you find her? Is she alive?"

"Yes she's alive – just, we had better get her inside and see if we can wake her up." They carried Alice over to Middlebrooks's hut and laid her down on a bed.

"Oh my God, Alice!" exclaimed Anna.

"We found her on a track about two hundred miles north-east of here," said Katlin. "We rescued her just in time before a pack of dogs got her."

"She needs hydrating," said Middlebrook filling a cup with water, "sit her up please Katlin."

Middlebrook held the cup to Alice's lips and managed to pour some liquid into her mouth. A few seconds later, Alice was coughing and spluttering as she became conscious.

"It's alright Alice, it's Barny and Anna," he soothed, "you're safe now."

Walking out of the tent Katlin was approached by Ed. "Do you know her?"

"She was one of our group who went on the raid. I wasn't sure if it was her at first." Katlin was being economical with the truth.

"Why didn't you tell me?"

"Well I'm telling you now," said Katlin starting to get annoyed. Then she walked off to give Joe the news.

Twenty-four hours later Alice was strong enough to look outside of the hut. She still ached badly from her ordeal but Middlebrook as ever was there to support her.

"Barny can I see Joe now?"

Middlebrook had told Alice about Joe earlier that day and now she couldn't wait to see him.

As Middlebrook helped Alice over to Joe's hut, Joe appeared in the doorway with a slightly skewed smile on his face. He was holding a stick in his right arm for support and Alice, barely noticing it, rushed the last few steps to give him a hug.

"I thought you wouldn't make it," said Alice unable to stop the tears from flowing.

"You can thank the Doc for that," replied Joe in a slow slightly slurred voice, "I didn't think I would see you again either."

They both hobbled into Joe's hut and Middlebrook walked away to give them some privacy.

The next day Middlebrook caught up with Alice. "We need to talk," he said, "are you up to telling me what happened to you?"

Alice nodded and proceeded to tell Middlebrook what happened from the moment she was captured to waking up here two days earlier.

Middlebrook listened intently, occasionally raising his eye brows in surprise at various moments. "You're lucky to be alive," he said finally.

Ignoring the comment Alice asked, "Barny, the voices I heard, am I going schizo?"

Middlebrook gave the question some consideration. "Schizophrenics don't open doors with their minds. Someone obviously let you out."

He wasn't sure if he believed his own answer; with Alice's track record, who knows what she is capable of.

"You say you were asleep when the door opened."

Alice nodded and started to cry. She leant on Middlebrook's shoulder and said, "They took my baby, Barny – I don't even know if it's a boy or a girl."

Middlebrook put a comforting arm around her and then it occurred to him. An idea that was too incredible to even consider. Did Alice's baby talk to her and open the door? Was there some kind of psychic connection? He decided to keep that theory to himself, at least for the time being.

"This may not be the best time to tell you but Anna had baby girl six weeks ago," he said tentatively.

Alice wiped her eyes and asked, "What's her name?"

"Marianne."

"That's pretty," sniffed Alice, "can I see her."

"Are you sure?"

Alice nodded and Middlebrook took her over to his and Anna's hut. "I've brought Alice over to see the baby," he said on entering the hut.

Anna wasn't sure if it was a good idea but realised that Alice was going to have to see her sooner or later. Anna picked the baby up out of her cot. Marianne was wrapped in a blanket and still fast asleep.

"Would you like to hold her?" offered Anna.

Alice nodded and sat down on a log which served as a stool, to receive the baby. Anna passed Marianne over to Alice and she cradled the child in her arms.

"Well look at you," said Alice in a soothing trembling voice, "you're beautiful. Aren't you just the sweetest thing?"

Alice's emotions got the better of her and she stood up and handed the baby to Middlebrook, then ran outside and burst into a flood of uncontrollable tears. Anna followed her out and held her. She understood that there was no real way of consoling Alice and that she had to just try and get it out of her system.

The next day Alice was sat on a bench drinking some tea, watching Joe. It was an unusually warm day for March, but a sadness hung over her like a storm cloud. She could hear a fast-flowing river in the distance and guessed that it was where they got their water from.

Joe had taken it upon himself to look after the animals and was doing his rounds, limping round with his walking stick. Alice had tried to help him but he just got bad tempered and impatient, so Alice left him to it. She wondered where Katlin was as she hadn't had a chance to talk to her since she arrived.

Middlebrook approached with Anna holding the baby. He sat down next to Alice.

"I'm just taking Marianne for some air," said Anna, "I'll see you later."

"Don't stray too far," said Middlebrook. He turned and smiled at Alice. "Joe's doing a great job with the animals – considering."

"Yes he looks in his element."

Alice looked at Middlebrook and enquired, "What happened, Barny – when the surviving trucks got back?"

Middlebrook drew a deep breath and said, "It was pretty chaotic that evening and the next day was no better…"

* * *

"I think we should evacuate this area as soon as possible," urged Katlin, "the Black Eyes will be looking for us."

It was mid-morning the next day after the raid and Middlebrook was trying to ascertain what the best treatment for Joe would be.

"Before we go anywhere we need to make Joe stable," insisted Middlebrook.

"What do you need?" enquired Katlin.

"What we need is a hospital," said Anna, knowing that it was out of the question.

"What about a vet's surgery?" suggested Katlin. "We could use Joe's back in town."

Anna and Middlebrook looked each other and nodded.

"Excellent idea," said Middlebrook, "let's get him loaded immediately."

Still unconscious, Joe was loaded into the back of the Range Rover with one half of the rear seats folded down. Middlebrook drove whilst Anna sat in the rear keeping a close eye on Joe.

"Joe's surgery is off a side road on Main Street," said Katlin.

Middlebrook drove as fast as he dare and soon they were entering Arrow Creek.

"It's just to the right down there," said Katlin pointing to a side street.

They pulled up outside the surgery and broke down the door. Katlin looked around nervously; she wasn't happy with the noise that they were making. With the door open, they wasted no time in carrying Joe inside and laying him on the operating table.

"What do you think Anna?" enquired Middlebrook.

Anna's experience of surgery, though not extensive, was better than Middlebrooks's. She inspected the wound and said finally, "Well the gap is small enough to allow the bone to regrow. He may need some debridement and repair of the meninges as best as possible. Then all we can do is close the wound. The biggest danger will be infection."

"What's debridement and meninges?" asked an alarmed Katlin.

We need to remove any damaged tissue and any other nasties we might find in there, that's all," said Middlebrook, in an attempt to reassure her.

"The meninges is a protective layer separating the brain from the scull." He continued, deliberately simplifying his explanation to save time.

"It must make a change to be working on the outside of the brain as opposed to what's in it – eh Doc?" Katlin joked. She was nervous and was struggling to deal with the situation.

Middlebrook smiled back at her and then he and Anna walked over to a sink to scrub up.

The procedure took over an hour but finally Joe was bandaged up and ready to be moved again. All through the operation he remained asleep which made their job easier.

"See if we can find some antibiotics and anti-seizure drugs. Just in case – oh and some pain killers would be useful too," said Anna.

When they arrived back at the base the remaining crew had just finished burying the soldier who had shot himself.

Corporal Ed Mitchell approached them as all three got out of the Range Rover.

"We need to decide what we are going to take," he said. "I've done a tally up and there are eleven of us left: four women and seven men. Vehicles amount to five trucks, two Humvee's, the 4x4 and a pick-up. I'm assuming we'll be leaving the RV behind."

Middlebrook nodded; it was a shame, the RV had been their home for a while now and he was going to miss it.

"What do you think, Corporal?" enquired Middlebrook.

"I think that we should take the minimum, sir," said Mitchell. "Three trucks, one Humvee and the 4x4."

"Good enough," replied Middlebrook, surprised to be addressed as sir, "load as much food, fuel and weapons as you can. We need to be out of here by dusk."

"Will it be safe to move Joe, do you think?" asked Anna.

"We have little choice," stated Middlebrook, "we'll keep him in the Range Rover, with plenty of bedding around him – he should be okay."

Katlin went with Corporal Mitchell to help pack up, and eventually by nightfall the small convoy moved out for pastures new.

* * *

"We kept to the tracks as much as we could," said Middlebrook, "and settled here about a week later. Joe woke up the next day after we had fixed him up.

He had a thumping headache, but at least he was conscious at last."

"The injury has affected him badly," said Alice, her eyes welling up again, "he isn't the same man."

"No," agreed Middlebrook emphatically, "though he's much improved. When he first woke up he couldn't stand and his speech was badly impaired. Joe has worked hard to improve."

Alice stood up and said, "Thanks Barny, you've always been there for me. What would I do without you?"

Middlebrook smiled and shrugged. "You would have coped somehow. It's a simple choice between survival and giving up."

Alice smiled and walked away; she needed some time to think so she found a spot under a tree in the corner of a field and contemplated her next move. She cast her mind back to England and all that had been taken away from her: John and her first child; her marriage and family. Then more recently there was Joe, a pale shadow of his former self, and the baby cut out of her. A sense of outrage overwhelmed Alice and eventually a steadfast resolve came over her. There would be no more tears. Those freaks had brought enough grief upon her and soon, if she had her way, it will be payback time. Alice decided to go and find Katlin.

The settlement had a small flock of sheep in a separate field nearby and a few of the ewes were close to giving birth. Alice found Katlin keeping an eye on them. It was a picture of pastoral serenity which made it difficult to believe that there had been a cataclysmic event on a global scale.

"I didn't have you down as a shepherd," said Alice breezily.

"It keeps me out of mischief," said Katlin.

Katlin was sitting near a tree and Alice approached and sat by her. "I haven't had a chance to thank you for rescuing me."

"That's okay, to be honest I came very close to leaving you there."

"Why didn't you?"

"Because I'm not a bitch," she continued, "and besides, what you went through to escape was pretty impressive. I'm not sure that I could've done it. There's more about you than I thought. You're okay."

"High praise indeed," chuckled Alice, "who knows in another life you and I might have been friends."

They looked at each other and said in unison, "Nah!" Both laughed at this and eventually they fell silent.

"You and me are too different," said Katlin not unreasonably.

Alice paused and then said, "Katlin, when you packed up and came here, did you bring those two green rucksacks."

"The nukes you mean?" Katlin replied, "of course we did. It would've been stupid to leave them for the Black Eyes to find. There was also a metal case with some weird looking guns in. Joe told me to leave them alone. Why do you ask?"

Alice looked at Katlin with steely determination and said, "I'm going back."

"Back where?"

"To the base where I was held captive, and I'm taking one of those nukes with me."

"You're going to nuke the base?" said Katlin incredulously.

Alice shook her head. "No, I'm going to take it through their time portal. I'm going to nuke their future."

"That's suicide," gasped Katlin.

"Not necessarily," replied Alice coolly, "but if that's what it takes then so be it."

CHAPTER TEN
THE BLINK OF AN EYE

Joe laid out a map of the area on the table in his hut. Alice had told him of her intentions to take a Nuclear device into the Deviants' future world, and had tried, without success, to talk her out of it. He never had any real influence over her and now he simply didn't have the energy or the willpower to argue the point. If he couldn't dissuade her, then he was going to do all he could to ensure that her mission was successful.

"So we are here," said Joe placing a finger on the map, "where do you think the Black Eye's base is?"

His slurred speech was difficult to understand sometimes and Alice had to concentrate hard to follow him; she scanned the map for land marks that might help her.

"There was a lot of forest, and I know the base was near a river, I remember hearing it when I escaped."

Studying the map for a little longer, Alice's finger alighted on the map.

"Here," she said decisively, "I think."

"You think? I need you to be sure."

"Yes I'm sure," she said finally after giving the map a second look.

"If you are right, then the Deviant base is only sixty miles away and what's more this is the same river that we use."

"Are you telling me that I was that close," said an incredulous Alice, "I must have travelled at least twice that distance."

"Yeah, you just went in the wrong direction. It's lucky for you that Katlin disobeyed orders and patrolled out further than agreed, or you would never have been found."

Alice simply nodded – there was no arguing the fact.

Middlebrook barged into the hut and made them jump. He knew something was going on and now he was angry.

"I've just found out from Katlin what you're planning, are you mad?" Middlebrook hated using words referring to insanity out of context, especially with one of his former patients, but on this occasion he felt it entirely appropriate.

"Look Barny we have to do something," pleaded Alice, "can you think of a better way to knock them out?"

"Okay, if you got through it might just work, but trying this on your own will be suicidal," said Middlebrook.

"She won't be going alone – I'm going with her."

They all looked round to see Katlin at the door. She looked at their dumbfounded expressions and smiled. "So, what's the plan?" she said and walked in to study the map.

"Are you sure about this?" asked Alice.

"Yeah, of course; we've got two backpacks so if we gonna nuke them one time then why not make it two times."

It seemed perfectly logical to Alice who simply smiled and nodded her agreement. Middlebrook, realising that he wasn't going to talk them out of it, gave up and left the hut. Alice followed after him.

"I know you hate violence," she said catching up with him, "but it's the only way. At least wish us luck."

"Of course I wish you luck, you're heading into a vipers' nest and I'm scared that we won't see you again."

Alice gave him a reassuring hug. "Don't worry, haven't you realised by now, I'm indestructible."

* * *

Later that day Alice and Katlin sorted out what clothes they were going to wear. The Deviant uniform was predominantly black so they dug out all the black clothes they had. Eventually, there they stood in Katlin's hut and examined each other's attire. Alice was wearing knee-length black boots, black leggings and a black T-shirt. Katlin decided on black trainers, black leggings also, and a black sweatshirt.

"I think you look more convincing, "said Alice, "you're slimmer than me."

Before Katlin could reply, there came a knock at the door. Katlin opened it and let Joe in. He sat down on a chair to rest and then said, "I had a whip around for these. Try them on."

He handed over a black balaclava hat and dark wraparound sunglasses to each of them and they duly put them on. The sunglasses mimicked the Deviant's Black Eyes closely and Katlin turned to look at herself in a mirror. She turned to Alice and grinned.

"This is excellent," she said with enthusiasm.

"At least from a distance," said Alice more cautiously, checking herself out in the mirror, "we might just get away with it."

"We need to go through the procedure with the bombs," said Joe, "you will both need to know how to arm them and set the timer."

Five minutes later Katlin was carrying a backpack and Alice was lugging a metal case. They entered Katlin's hut to see Joe still there waiting patiently.

"She insisted on bringing it," said Katlin.

"Of course, these ray guns are brilliant.

"Ray guns?" mocked Joe, "this isn't Flash Gordon you know."

"What would you call them then?"

Joe chuckled and shrugged, realising that after all it really didn't matter. Both Alice and Katlin chuckled back; they hadn't seen Joe laugh in a long time.

First they worked out how to arm and time the bomb. Joe made them run through it several times until he was certain that they were confident. There would be no room or time for error. Any mistake would prove disastrous. Then Joe's attention turned to the metal box. He opened it to reveal the four remaining weapons. Katlin looked in, fascinated.

"Alice, show her how they work."

Alice picked up one of the guns and handed it to Katlin. "Take it but don't hold the grip just yet." Then Alice pulled out a gun for herself. "Let's go outside and test them out."

As they walked out to the side of the hut, Joe stood at the door to watch.

"Watch this," said Alice.

She put her hand to the grip and the gun sprang into life. Just like before, metal panels extended up her forearm and locked on.

"What the hell?" said Katlin.

"That's not all, watch this." Alice raised the gun and fired a laser beam at a tree. The thin yellow beam burnt a hole in the trunk and splinters of bark broke off in all directions.

"How did you do that?" said an amazed Katlin examining her own gun. "The thing hasn't got a trigger."

"That's the best thing about it – it works by thought. Try it."

Katlin tentatively held the grip and then flinched as the metal panels became part of her arm.

"Now point it at the tree and think shoot."

Katlin did so and a beam hit the tree close to Alice's shot and made a deep hole in the trunk. "Whoa!" exclaimed Katlin deeply impressed, "how do I get it off again."

"Just think *release*."

Again Katlin did so and the gun shut down into standby mode.

"This is awesome," said Katlin, we're definitely taking these."

"This gun is configured to you and you only," said Joe to both of them, "so don't get them mixed up."

Later they marked the backpacks with their names and gaffer taped the laser guns to the side. Joe found them a long length of rope and a pair of walkie-talkies then finally they were ready to go.

* * *

Corporal Ed Mitchell volunteered to take them the following evening and he loaded the two bombs onto the Range Rover ready for the journey. Soon they were on their way to the agreed drop off point five miles out from the Deviant base.

Both sat in the back thinking of the people they had just left behind. The goodbyes to Joe, Barny and Anna had been especially emotional for Alice. For the first time ever she thought that she saw a tear in Barny's eye, and wondered if she would ever see them again. Katlin was having similar thoughts and turned to look at Alice.

Alice took her hand and said, "I'm glad you're coming with me. I don't think I would have swung it without you."

"Wild horses wouldn't have stopped me," smiled Katlin.

For the rest of the journey they sat in silence, only occasionally giving Ed directions from the map.

Ninety minutes later Ed pulled the jeep up to a halt. "This is as far as I go," he said.

"Thanks Ed," said Alice leaning forwards and giving him a peck on the cheek. Then she got out and went to the back to remove the backpacks.

Katlin got out and moved across to the driver's door. She opened it, stepped up and kissed Ed passionately on the lips.

"Thanks Ed," she said with a grin. "Take care of yourself."

"You too," was all he could muster, as he watched Katlin go and help Alice put the backpacks on and disappear into the night, then said quietly to himself, with a heavy heart, "and it's Corporal Mitchell, God dammit."

Eventually he started the jeep and drove home.

* * *

"Which way?" whispered Katlin.

Alice was studying a compass and responded by pointing in the right direction. Slowly but steadily they bushwhacked through the forest, taking care to make as little noise as possible. The backpacks were heavy but the straps were thick and well-padded so they were able to manage the weight reasonably without too much effort.

Two hours later they were close to the tree line and Alice could hear the river. "Just beyond the trees is a stretch of open ground that leads straight to the base," Alice said.

"How far do you think?"

Alice shrugged, "Oh – maybe quarter of a mile or so."

Stealthily they crept out of the woodland and steadfastly approached the Deviant base. To one side the half dome of the time portal loomed a short distance away.

"They look massive close up," gasped Katlin.

Alice ignored her; she was looking for the vent which she dropped out of when making her escape. Eventually she found it and couldn't believe the grille had not been repaired, finding it lying in the grass where she had discarded it.

"This is lucky, they obviously didn't know how I escaped." Alice took off her backpack and Katlin following her lead did the same.

"This is what we are going to have to do," instructed Alice, "along this vent is a ninety degree bend and then the pipe rises vertically about fifty feet. I'll go first and take the rope, you attach a bomb and I'll pull it up."

Katlin nodded and watched as Alice laid on her back with the rope tied around her waist and then entered the vent. Katlin could hear the sound of Alice scrabbling along the tunnel as it echoed back to her. She tied one bomb to the other end of the rope and placed it in the vent. The wait seemed agonisingly long then suddenly the backpack started shifting down the tunnel. Katlin followed behind knowing that she would have to retrieve the end of the rope when Alice dropped it down again. Soon both bombs were up with Alice and all that remained was for Katlin to negotiate the shaft. She laid on her back and pushed herself along the horizontal section until she got to the bend. The shaft was tight and made it difficult to manoeuvre but she managed to get her arms above her to use the ribbing around the shaft to pull and push up with. Eventually she was up with Alice and they were moving as quietly as they could along the complex venting system.

"Wait," whispered Alice, "I need to get my bearings."

Alice looked around her and tried to remember the route that she took. There were three side junctions and Alice had to think through the route backwards from the time before.

"This way," she eventually whispered and took a junction to the left.

It wasn't long before they reached what for Alice was the familiar ladder which led down to the corridor. It was time to don the balaclava and sunglasses.

"We need to get down to ground level," whispered Alice again pushing the ladder back up into the vent. "It's one or maybe two floors down."

Katlin nodded and followed as Alice moved off looking for a way down.

An overwhelming urge came over Alice as she thought about her baby, to attempt a rescue, but put the thought to the back of her mind. The mission was more important. The corridor very soon terminated at an elevator and spiral staircase leading both up and down.

"Which shall we take?" enquired Alice.

"The stairs, we don't want to be cornered in an elevator."

Good enough, thought Alice and they made their way down the stairs to ground level. Quickly they moved to hide by a side wall, they could see out onto the docking point on the landing apron and it was busy with Black Eyes going about their business.

"We need to get on one of those crafts which are going out," whispered Alice, "what do you think?"

Nodding, Katlin peaked out form their vantage point. Several vessels were parked up and it was difficult to tell which ones were heading out. Then Katlin noticed one a little further down the row being loaded with metal crates.

"I think I've found one, look for yourself. It's the fifth one down."

Swapping positions with Katlin, Alice sneaked a look. Sure enough there was one vessel being loaded up for the trip back through the portal. Unfortunately it was being overseen by two Black Eyes. They decided to bide their time and wait for right moment to act.

Eventually two more Black Eyes arrived dressed in a manner which suggested that they were the crew. They spoke to the first pair who had just completed the loading process, who then moved off. Finally, as the crew were boarding the vessel, Alice and Katlin made their move. They ran down the jetty and stumbled through the closing door of the vessel just as it slammed shut behind them. Both Black Eyes heard the commotion and the co-pilot decided to check the cargo compartment while the pilot navigated the vessel away from its docking point. As he entered, Katlin came up behind him and shoved her gun under his chin.

"Back into the cabin – don't try anything, it'll give me great pleasure to kill you."

They entered the cabin to the alarm of the pilot. He could see the look of fear on his co-pilot's face. Alice pointed her gun at the pilot and said, "Just carry on as normal and you might just live through this."

"They're bluffing," said the pilot in a mocking tone, "they need us."

With that Katlin gave off a short burst from her laser gun. The beam went up through the Deviant's chin and out through the top of his head, hitting the padded lining of the roof. The Deviant dropped to the floor, his large lifeless eyes staring at the ceiling. Then Katlin turned to the pilot.

"You were saying?" she said, now pointing the gun at him.

Having two guns trained on him, the pilot said no more but got on with the business of flying the craft. With no windows, they watched the video screen as the vessel started to make its way towards the time portal.

"What are you intentions?" asked the nervous pilot.

"I could tell you," whispered Katlin in his ear, "but then I'd have to kill you."

Overhearing, Alice just smiled.

In no time at all they were approaching the huge gateway and as they entered, all that they could see on the screen was static. Suddenly the screen came back to life and displayed a huge, brightly lit docking bay filled with vessels coming and going.

"Follow your usual procedure," said Alice, "and when you stop open the door."

The Deviant docked his craft and opened a side access door which led onto a gangway. The pilot turned his head to look at Katlin, but before he could say anything, Alice shot him through the temple and the Deviant flopped lifelessly over his instrument panel.

"Oh – I lied, we were going to kill you anyway," she said with as much contempt in her voice as she could muster.

"Come on," urged Katlin, "we won't have much time before they are discovered."

Both made their way along the gangway as fast as they dare, not wanting to attract attention to themselves. A short distance further and they were into a short corridor that led to an antechamber with several passages leading off of it.

"Which one do we take?" asked Katlin.

"How the hell do I know, I think it's time for us to split up."

"I'll take this one," said Katlin nodding.

Alice chose another passage and said, "Switch your walkie-talkie on; we'll need to stay in contact."

Katlin disappeared down one corridor and Alice did the same. Katlin walked down several passages working purely on guesswork, until eventually she entered another antechamber. This one was different however, on one side was one passage and on the other side was a large glass screen looking down on an area which looked to Katlin like the centre of operations. The area was busy with Deviants and Katlin ducked down below the glass to avoid being discovered. She took out her walkie-talkie and spoke to Alice.

"It looks like I've found their main control centre. This could be a good place to plant my bomb."

"Okay," puffed Alice. The backpack was starting to get heavy now and Alice was starting to feel it. "I'm going to get as far away from you as I dare. I'll get back to you when I'm ready to synchronise timers."

Signing off, Katlin settled down to wait for Alice's call.

After fifteen minutes walking, Alice's pace had slowed dramatically, it didn't help that the corridors were uncomfortably warm and as she stopped to catch her breath, she looked around for options. A little further down Alice saw an opening different to all the others she had seen. Approaching it cautiously she noticed that it wasn't another corridor and was darkened. She edged in and was confronted with strips of a plastic type material hanging from the ceiling. Pushing them to one side, Alice walked into an area that was even warmer and almost pitch black. She removed her sunglasses and balaclava. Moving along a wall a few steps, she was suddenly startled by a light which came on somewhere above her. The room was still poorly lit but she could now see opposite her what looked like some kind of enclosure fixed against the wall. Removing her backpack, Alice walked towards it. The enclosure was about four feet high and two feet wide. The front was curved and as Alice got closer she could see it was made of glass or a Perspex type material. Putting her face close to the glass Alice could just make out through the slight condensation a young girl: a human girl. The image looked all too familiar to Alice as she observed tubes entering the girl's body, especially the swollen abdomen, and wires attached at various points. The enclosure was clearly too short for her and as Alice looked down at the bottom of the poor girl's entombment she realised to her horror that her legs had been amputated. Alice gave a gasp and put a hand up to her mouth in shock, then peered in closer again to see how far into her pregnancy she was. As Alice observed, the closed eyes of the girl snapped open wide and gave Alice another shock.

She recoiled, and her staggered movement triggered a number of lights which illuminated the whole cavernous chamber. Alice stared at the sight in front of her. She couldn't believe what she saw. The girl's cocoon was only one of many. Rows and rows of cocoons ran down the chamber. She looked up and could see more rising as far as the eye could see: hundreds – thousands of them. The horror of what lay in front of her suddenly dawned on Alice. All these wretched young girls with their legs amputated to save space, artificially impregnated, their embryo's genetically manipulated and imprisoned in what to her looked like a living death. She felt a wave of nausea come over her and she knelt on all fours and vomited. Alice coughed and spluttered, then came to her senses. She took out her walkie-talkie and contacted Katlin.

"I've found a good place for my bomb," she said, her voice shaking, "let's arm them."

"Are you alright?" enquired a concerned Katlin.

"Yeah, let's just synchronise the timers and get out of here."

With the bombs armed and the timers set for thirty minutes, Alice started to make her way back, hoping that she would be able to find Katlin.

* * *

"When were they found?" said a clearly incensed Mida, who was now looking down on the two dead pilots.

"About twenty minutes before you got here," said a nervous Nih-trooper.

"Get your men together," ordered Mida, "this is a serious breach of security. I want whoever did this found, and quick."

"They could be anywhere in this maze of corridors," said the trooper.

Mida acknowledged this point and said to herself, "Where are intruders likely to head for?"

Then it dawned on her, "The Control Centre. Get your men, quick."

The trooper saluted and disappeared to rally his troops. Soon they were heading down the corridor looking for the intruders.

Whilst Katlin impatiently waited for Alice to turn up, she suddenly heard some movement that couldn't possibly have been Alice: the sound of several boots came echoing down the passageway towards her. She peeked around the wall expecting Deviants to appear any second and when they did she shot a beam straight at them. It was a group of about fifteen Nih-troopers and Mida. Katlin hit the first trooper in the chest and he fell to the floor. Killed instantly. The rest quickly retreated around a corner, out of the line of fire.

Katlin got back onto her walkie-talkie. "Alice you'd better get here quick I'm under attack."

"I'll be there as soon as I know where you are," puffed Alice, hurrying as fast as she could.

As Katlin kept a watchful eye on the Nih-troopers, a laser beam came shooting down the other corridor and burnt a chunk out of her right thigh. With a scream of pain shooting up her leg, she turned and shot up the other corridor, hitting the trooper and forcing the other three to back off.

"Alice I've been hit," she grimaced, "they've got me in the leg."

"Hold on I'm close," reassured Alice. She had heard the commotion and had headed straight to where the noise was coming from. As Alice got closer, she peered round a corner. There she saw three troopers helping another that Katlin had wounded. Stepping out suddenly, Alice gave out several blasts and killed all three. Then as she approached the wounded trooper, he tried to raise his gun. Alice gave him a fatal blast and stepped over the bodies to try and reach Katlin. After seeing what they had done to those poor girls, Alice had no compassion for them whatsoever. As far as she was concerned the only good Black Eye was a dead one.

Hearing someone coming down the second passage, Katlin trained her gun and then gave a mental sigh of relief when she saw that it was Alice. Katlin put her hand up to tell Alice to stop at the junction. If she tried to walk across the antechamber the Nih-troopers would surely kill her. Then Katlin pointed up the first corridor to indicate where the enemy was. Alice understood and then noticed that Katlin was lying against the wall with a nasty gash in her right thigh.

"Cover me," whispered Alice, "I'm coming over."

Nodding, Katlin leant out and started shooting again, and as she did so Alice made a dash across. A shaft of yellow laser fire just missed her as she ran over to Katlin and slid across the floor unharmed. She turned to examine Katlin's wound.

"That looks nasty," winced Alice, "can you walk?"

"I can't even stand up on my own," grimaced Katlin.

Alice looked at the timer on Katlin's backpack. It showed that there was just over twelve minutes left.

"This is the hurt locker Alice. We're not getting out of here," said a pragmatic Katlin noticing the timer as well. Alice had reached the same conclusion. They needed more time but dared not set the bombs to detonate any later, as they might be discovered. Alice sat against the wall next to Katlin and put a reassuring arm around her.

"Well if we must die, then I can't think of a better reason than saving the planet," she smiled.

Katlin smiled back but it was little consolation.

Mida watched as the human dashed across the antechamber and recognised her instantly. "Alice!" she hissed, relishing the opportunity to finally kill her, "got you at last."

After several more minutes of enduring the stand-off, Mida decided to take the initiative.

"Alice there's no need for any more unpleasantness," shouted Mida in a reasonable tone, "let's talk."

"She knows you?" said Katlin.

"Yeah," replied Alice sardonically, "we're old acquaintances."

"What is there to say?" shouted Alice.

"Look, I want you to know that I am unarmed and I'm going to make my way towards you. Let's be sensible about this."

With one of them wounded, Mida felt that she had a good chance of getting the upper hand. She still had the knife on her belt, hidden behind her back. Alice watched closely as Mida cautiously walked down to the antechamber.

"Help me up," Katlin grimaced, "I don't want her to see me lying here like this."

Alice got Katlin to her feet but she had to lean on Alice for support. They checked the timer. Two minutes left. When Mida turned the corner she saw the two girls arm in arm, one clearly in severe pain. She smiled at them.

"This is silly," she simpered, "why don't you give yourselves up?"

"What would be the point, we have already beaten you," replied Alice.

Puzzled by this reply, Mida frowned. "Don't be absurd," she mocked.

Alice gestured to the backpack on the ground. The timer read ninety seconds.

"What is it?" said Mida, clearly alarmed.

"It's a nuclear bomb," smiled Alice, "we've set two."

"No – no!" cried Mida in anger and then in terror slumped against the wall. Realising that there was no point in trying to run, she slid down the wall and said quietly, "this isn't happening. You stupid bitch."

"Time to make peace with your God," said Alice, knowing that their time was nearly up, "if you have one that is."

Mida looked again at the timer in sheer horror – only five seconds left.

Still standing, Alice and Katlin hugged each other tightly.

"Goodbye Alice," said Katlin.

Alice closed her eyes and said, "See you on the other side."

As the timer counted down to zero, oblivion came in the blink of an eye and three suns rose high in the heat of midday.

CHAPTER ELEVEN
THE PROPERTY OF ALICE DENHAM

The Range Rover pulled up on a slight incline. It was early afternoon with a heavily overcast sky. The smoke rising from the expanse of ground laid out ahead, just added to the harrowing gloom of what the occupants beheld in front of them. Cars and trucks were still burning and the only light emanating from the Deviant base were the flames rising up and licking the sky. It had been a week since Alice and Katlin had infiltrated the base and when their power suddenly shut down, a fierce battle ensued as humans took the opportunity to attack.

Ed Mitchell, Cristian Rogers – a private in General Jackson's company –and Middlebrook, who insisted on coming, got out and looked over the depressing scene. The stench of smoke, burning oil and death hung heavy in the air as they saw all the dead bodies, mostly human, and some Deviant.

"They were slaughtered." commented Cristian shaken by the sight.

"The Black Eye's fire power must have been too much for them." said Middlebrook with sadness.

"Well they must've given them a bloody nose." replied Ed gesturing towards the damaged Deviant base.

"It doesn't look like it's fully knocked out though," observed Middlebrook, "but it won't take them long to get those flames under control."

Suddenly their ears pricked up to a faint sound drifting up from the battlefield. Cristian didn't hesitate; he rushed over to where the sound had come from.

"Wait," hissed Middlebrook, "you'll be too exposed out there."

"We can't just ignore it," quipped Ed.

Middlebrook sighed and followed Ed who had started to catch up with Cristian. The voice was located in the middle of the battlefield: a man badly shot up and moaning due to his severe wounds. Middlebrook finally caught up and knelt to see how bad the man was. He didn't look good, there was a big gash out of his left side just above the waist and his left arm was severed just below the elbow.

Kneeling by his head, Cristian raised him up to give him some water from his canteen. The man responded and drank a little, wincing with pain as he tried to swallow.

"What's your name soldier?" enquired Ed.

"J-J- Jameson," whispered the man barely able to speak, "David Jameson.

All three moved closer to hear him.

"Can you tell us what happened?" asked Middlebrook.

Jameson summoned what strength he had left and said, "When we saw that the power had shut down at the base we mobilised all the men and fire power we had and executed a surprise attack." He paused for a moment to summon up the energy to continue. "They were ready for us. We didn't stand a chance. It was futile."

"Don't say that," said Cristian with emotion in his voice, "it was a brave thing you did here. It's just the beginning."

Jameson had exhausted what energy he had left and finally closed his eyes. With a gentle exhale of breath, his head rolled to one side and he lay there, silent and still.

Middlebrook was starting to get very edgy, exposed as they were in the middle of the battleground. "He's gone," he said with compassion, "we need to go – there's nothing we can do for him now."

Ed grabbed Cristian's arm to encourage him to move and they stood up to make their way back to the jeep. Middlebrook took one last look at the burning base. The smoke had cleared slightly and now he could see the massive semi-circular sphere. It was devoid of all power and having rolled over, was lying at an awkward angle like a giant discarded pudding bowl.

"There must be scenes like this all over the country – all over the world." reflected Middlebrook realising the scale of suffering which lay around him. Then he thought of the person culpable for all this mayhem.

"Goodbye Alice, I'll miss you," he said with deep sadness, knowing she and Katlin died in some obscure place and time purely for the benefit of all mankind.

Then all three sullenly picked their way back to the jeep for the journey home.

* * *

Standing in the doorway of her hut, Anna holding her baby in her arms, was sick with worry: Middlebrook and the others where hours overdue. Eventually all three came walking into the settlement. Anna put Marianne in the cot and then rushed out to meet Middlebrook.

"Thank God," she said hugging him, "I've been so worried. What happened? Where's the Range Rover?"

"It ran out of fuel about five miles away," replied Middlebrook, tired from his exertion.

The other two drifted off to get something to eat.

Noticing that he was tired Anna said, "Come on, you must be starving."

Middlebrook nodded, followed her in and sat down. He could see that she was eager for news and he was not in the mood to talk but knew however that it would be unfair, so he waited for Anna's bombardment of questions.

Anna could see that he was hungry and thirsty, so decided to sit quietly and let him eat and rest a while.

Presently, Middlebrook was feeling better and decided to tell Anna about their day of exploration. Anna listened intently to his story and then got up to see to Marianne who had just started to cry.

"What does this mean? Are the Black Eyes gone? Are all our people dead?"

"It's impossible to say for sure, We didn't see any activity at the base but I'm sure there must still be Black Eyes in there. As for people – who knows?"

There was a knock at the door and Anna opened it to see Joe standing there leaning on his walking stick. He also was keen to hear any news but decided to wait and let Middlebrook rest before he dropped by.

Not wanting to go through the whole thing again, Middlebrook gave Joe a truncated version of the day's experiences.

"What about Alice and Katlin?" asked Joe, "any sign of them?"

"I'm afraid not, I think we will have to face the fact that they didn't make it back."

Joe sat there silently taking this in, and Middlebrook, after giving Anna a nervous glance continued, "There's something else you need to know. Alice was pregnant when she was captured on the raid."

Joe reeled at this news and started to stand up, clearly angry.

"We didn't tell you at first because we wanted you to get strong," pleaded Anna, "then as time went on it became harder and harder to find the right moment."

"I'm sorry Joe," said Middlebrook taking the blame, "I should have told you sooner."

With his mind racing, Joe left the hut and walked over to the field where the sheep were grazing. He sat down in the spot where Katlin liked to dwell and shouted out at the top of his voice. Joe felt alone now more than ever before. He had lost his wife and now Katlin and Alice, and finally a child that he knew nothing about. It was too much to bear, Joe put his hands to his face and wept.

* * *

Having been thrown into disarray by the human attack, the well-coordinated Deviant base was in chaos. The power had suddenly and for no apparent, shut down. Communication with the future had been completely cut-off. Isolated and more vulnerable now, the humans, at least those remaining that were able to fight, had rallied themselves for a surprise offensive.

DM Khai Drypha stood and watched as his junior officers ran around barking orders. Everyone was pitching in to try and get the base operational again. Satisfied that progress was being made, he decided to check on the baby crèche to make sure everything was in order. Much had been gambled on this operation being a success and he was keen to put his mind at rest.

When Drypha arrived at the crèche all seemed comparitively normal and serene. Rows and rows of cots could be seen being tended to by human carers. Drypha approached Karen Foster.

"Where's the child?" he enquired in a stern voice.

"Over here, sir," replied Karen knowing exactly which child he meant. "I thought it best to keep the others separate."

Karen led Drypha over to the cot and he looked down at the baby dispassionately. "Make sure no harm comes to this child. I will be holding you personally responsible."

"As you wish, sir," Karen acquiesced.

She hated the Devi's but knew that she had to bow to their will in order to survive. After the failed attempt to stop Middlebrook attending the meeting, Karen couldn't afford any more of what to the Deviants would be another mistake. Drypha left, satisfied that all was well, and when he was out of sight Karen picked up the baby and held it in her arms.

She looked down on the infant sleeping soundly, and realised that she had become quite attached to it in the few weeks since the birth. This was the closest that she was ever going to get to being a mother and Karen was determined that no harm would come to the child; even if she had to die in the process. While she sat on a chair gently rocking the baby, an idea came into her head: a plan, a desperate plan.

Later that day she managed to steel a guard's uniform. If her plan was going to work then she would have to look like a Devi as best as she could. In the chaos, security had become perfunctory and Karen knew that this would be her best and probably only chance.

* * *

In the early hours of the following morning a small group of soldiers, survivors from the attack, had positioned themselves just behind a ridge overlooking the battlefield. The objective was to ascertain what activity there was in the base and to see how the Black Eyes were coping.

"It's looking pretty dead out there, sir," said Private Hank Sanders.

Hank was a marksman and had a reputation as an excellent sniper. Now he was looking into the valley with a night vision device attached to the telescope of his Armalite AR-50 rifle.

Looking through his night vision binoculars Lieutenant Williams agreed. He scanned the base but could see no movement whatsoever.

"We're wasting our time here, Private," he said at last, "we'll give it a few more minutes and then call it a night."

Hank continued to scan the area and then his attention whipped to some movement close to the confines of the base.

"I've got something, sir," said Hank excitedly, "looks like a Black Eye carrying some kinda box. Close to the base."

Lieutenant Williams looked again and located the figure moving furtively but steadily towards the river.

"What are they doing?" he said, half to himself.

"Do you want me to shoot him?" enquired Hank.

"Not yet, let's see what he's up to."

The figure continued its progress to the river until eventually stopping at the river's edge.

Karen couldn't believe her luck: she had managed to sneak out with Alice's baby in an incubator. Carrying it with the baby inside proved to be awkward and cumbersome but keeping close to the base, circumventing the derelict sphere, she was determined to see her plan through. Eventually Karen made it to the river bank. The noise of the fast flowing river seemed almost alien to her, never having experienced it until she travelled back in time.

Placing the incubator on the river bank, Karen removed the lid and checked that everything was in place. The electronic tag was around the child's left wrist, the drip was attached to the right arm and the top vent was open to allow the baby to breath. She looked tenderly at the baby who was now staring back up at her.

"Goodbye my sweet," she said, and kissed the child on the forehead. Then she placed the lid in position and pressed a button on the side. A short hissing sound indicated that the incubator had sealed airtight except for the open vent on top.

As Karen waded into the fast flowing water she had no idea that a sniper's telescopic sight was trained on her. She placed the incubator into the water and pushed it away. It drifted into the darkness and Karen turned around to walk back to the shallows. As she stumbled on a stone a bullet whistled close by her and made a splash in the river. Karen barely noticed; the sniper was using a silencer.

"Damn I missed," said Hank in disbelief – he hardly ever missed. Hank loaded another bullet into the breech ready to take another shot.

Lieutenant Williams continued to watch as the figure scrambled up onto dry land and take off her helmet.

"Wait!" he said not believing what he saw, "it's not a Black Eye. It's a woman: a human woman."

Quickly he organised three of his troops to help him scout round to cut her off.

"Better be quick, sir," said Hank, "I've just sighted four Black Eyes running down to meet her."

"Right," said the lieutenant, "shoot them if you can, we're gonna try a rescue."

Karen stood up and heard the sound of feet marching, moving quickly towards her. "Crap," she said to herself, "they've found out already." She knew that it would cost her her life, but she'd hoped it would take a little longer to be discovered.

The guards approached her and one walked up, grabbed her by the arm and said, "This area is off limits to humans. You're under arrest. Come with me."

No sooner had he said it when a bullet hit him in the back and he dropped to the floor like a stone. The other three looked at each other initially confused, as was Karen. Then a second was hit in the back of the head. The bullet came out of his right eye and shattered his visor, splattering Karen with blood. The final two, panicking, tried to take cover, but not before Hank dispatched another. By now Lieutenant Williams was close enough to affect a rescue, and one of his men threw a knife and hit the final guard in the chest. He fell to the ground writhing in pain, wounded but not dead.

Completely bemused, Karen just stood there as the four soldiers approached her.

"Lieutenant Williams at your service ma'am," he said saluting.

A soldier ran past him and knelt at the wounded Deviant. Pulling out the knife, the Deviant gave out a cry. Then in a frenzied rage the soldier stabbed him repeatedly until the Deviant moved no more.

Karen stared at this display of brutality transfixed and appalled.

"That's Private Hughes ma'am," said the lieutenant matter-of-factly, "he really doesn't like Black Eyes. They took both of his daughters and killed his wife."

Karen nodded; she understood all too well the suffering they had gone through.

"What are you doing here?" enquired the lieutenant. "What was in the box?"

Not wanting the soldiers to retrieve the incubator and risk having the child killed, Karen decided to lie.

"It was my baby," she said, "it passed away and I wanted to give it a dignified send off."

The officer stared at Karen but said nothing. He wasn't convinced that she was telling the truth. Karen stared back, trying to brazen it out.

Private Hughes approached covered in Deviant blood. Distracted, the lieutenant realised that they had been standing there too long.

"It's time we high-tailed it outta here," he said. "If you wanna live I suggest you come with us."

Karen nodded eagerly, she hadn't bargained on a rescue.

"My name's Karen Foster," she said, "thank you, I would like that."

With that Lieutenant Williams took her by the arm and they disappeared quickly into the night.

* * *

Megan Cornell sat down for a moment on the river bank. It was her turn to fetch water but on such a warm and sunny day she stopped to enjoy the restful scenery. The river flowed past steadily with a shimmering light as the sun reflected off it. The only thing spoiling the tranquillity however was Cristian Rogers who had insisted on accompanying her.

Cristian had picked a length of grass and started to gently brush it across Megan's cheek. Jolted out of her reverie, she brushed the grass away from her cheek and said, "What are you doing here?" in and irritated tone.

She knew exactly why he had come. For some time now Megan had suspected that he was attracted to her and she was flattered. At twenty-four, Cristian was two years younger than her, and under normal circumstances she would have preferred someone slightly older. But these were not normal circumstances; the pickings back at the settlement were slim and Cristian was for her, the most eligible. In her mind practicality had overridden any thoughts of romance.

Cristian shrugged, "I just thought you might like some help – some company."

Megan decided to take pity on him.

"That's thoughtful of you," she simpered and took his hand in hers, "I was just teasing."

Putting his hand up to her cheek, Cristian moved in for a kiss but Megan whipped her head round, alerted by a sound behind her.

"Did you hear that?" she said.

"No. What?"

"It came from over there. It sounded like a baby's cry."

"I didn't hear it,"

The cry came again, and alerted to the sound, Cristian heard it too.

"It came from over there." he said, pointing at a stretch of river bank.

They both stood up and walked in the direction of the sound until eventually they were looking down into the long grasses and reeds that were growing by the bank. There stuck in the undergrowth was a container. Cristian looked at Megan and then jumped in to retrieve it.

"Be careful."

"It looks like a baby. Here take it from me," said Cristian, passing the container up to her. Cristian scrambled back up onto the bank and Megan placed the container on the grass. They both peered in through the lid.

"Look at that." said Megan in amazement.

Staring back up at them was a baby with a quiff of blond hair and the biggest blue eyes they had ever seen. Megan was perturbed, the eyes were abnormally large.

"It's a Black Eye," bellowed Cristian noticing the eyes also.

"No – no it's not, the eyes may be large but they look human."

"Look at the pupils though," said Cristian.

Instead of being circular the pupil split the shimmering blue iris into three sections.

"We had better get it back to the settlement." decided Megan. With the incubator loaded onto the retrieved Range Rover they drove hastily back into camp.

As the jeep screeched to a halt Middlebrook turned round in alarm. An excited Megan got out and ran over to him.

"We've found something," she said excitedly.

Intrigued, Middlebrook walked round to the back of the jeep just as Cristian was lifting the incubator out.

"It's a baby Doc," said Cristian, "a baby."

Middlebrook looked in and could barely believe his eyes. "Where did you find it?"

"In the water by the riverbank caught up in some undergrowth," said Megan.

"Bring it into my hut," said Middlebrook.

Cristian carried the incubator in and set it down on a table.

"What have you got there?" enquired Anna.

"It appears to be a baby," he said casually, "found in the river."

Anna peered in and studied the infant closely. "My God look at those eyes," she asserted, "we can't leave it in here. Open the thing up."

Middlebrook looked around the incubator looking for some kind of catch until he noticed the button. With a gentle press there was a hiss and the lid popped open slightly. He removed the lid and recoiled at the smell.

"Phew – I think the baby needs changing," he gasped, "it must've been travelling downstream for days."

"Give it to me," said Anna impatiently as she lifted the child out.

Whilst cleaning the baby up, Anna turned to the others and said, "It's a boy."

"What's that round its wrist?" asked Middlebrook. "*His* wrist I mean."

He gently removed the tag and examined it closely. Without realising it he touched a sensor and a sentence lit up in green on the tag. Middlebrook read it out loud: "This baby is the property of Alice Denham."

Anna and Middlebrook looked at each other in amazement.

"What did they do to him?" said Anna, her hand over her mouth.

* * *

Later, Anna bathed and fed the baby boy and settled him down in the cot with Marianne.

"We're going to have to tell Joe," said Anna, "this is his child too."

Middlebrook hadn't thought of that but agreed that he needed to be told.

"I'll go and talk to him now." he said.

Events overtook him however, the news had travelled fast and Joe barged into their hut anxious to see the baby.

"Joe, I was just about to come over and talk to you."

"Let me see the child," slurred Joe.

Anna walked over to the cot and picked the boy up and Joe approached with apprehension. He stared at the child for an inordinately long time, observing the large blue eyes and then suddenly started to back off.

"No it can't be, this is not my son."

"This is Alice's baby," insisted Middlebrook. "And you're the father."

Joe simply shook his head and made a hasty exit.

"Well I didn't expect that," said Middlebrook.

"To suddenly find you have a son," observed Anna, "and for the child to look like this must be quite a shock for him. Give it time. He'll eventually come round."

The next day Middlebrook was nursing the baby. He couldn't help but notice how serene the child was. He looked up at Middlebrook with those hypnotic eyes and gave a faint smile.

"He's really quite beautiful," he said.

"We're going to have to give him a name," said Anna being practical.

"Got any ideas?"

"Yes," said Anna decisively. "We'll call him Joseph."

"Why?" enquired Middlebrook, surprised at her choice.

"Because it might help Joe to bond with him."

Anna sat down with Marianne cradled in her left arm and then held her right arm out to take Joseph. After handing him over, Middlebrook looked down taking in the sight: Anna with a baby in each arm. With dismay and sadness it dawned on him that in Marianne, his daughter, he was looking at the past. And in Joseph, Alice's son, he was looking at the future.

PART THREE

THE STAR CHILD

CHAPTER TWELVE
THE INVITATION

On the eve of Marianne's twenty-first birthday, Middlebrook was worried. Joseph had been gone on his excursion for over three weeks now and had promised Marianne that he would be back for their celebration. Without knowing when Joseph's exact birth date was, but knowing that it must be close to hers, they decided to make it the same day. Having grown up together, Marianne idolised Joseph, more the way a much younger sibling might. Middlebrook was not surprised at this, Joseph showed a maturity and intelligence way beyond his age – or any humans age for that matter. His abilities however went far beyond that.

Middlebrook cast his mind back to when Joseph was a baby. Before his first birthday, he recalls Anna telling him once that she distinctly remembers putting a bottle of milk on the table ready to give to Joseph, then turned her back to settle Marianne down and when she turned back again, Joseph had the bottle and was drinking in his cot. Anna could not explain how he had obtained the bottle. Middlebrook dismissed the incident at the time, assuming Anna to be mistaken, but eventually came to realise that Joseph had mental powers way beyond his comprehension.

At the age of one Joseph was talking fluently. By three he was reading and writing like an adult and at ten years of age Middlebrook was struggling intellectually to keep up with him. It wasn't until he was fifteen however, that Joseph's telekinesis and powers of telepathy began to become apparent. He could second guess anything anyone was about to say and liked to show off with it. Other members of the settlement found his behaviour to be unnerving and generally avoided him, so Middlebrook had to tell Joseph to tone it down and at least try and behave like a normal human being, even if strictly speaking, he wasn't one. Joseph's childhood had been somewhat isolated, being disinclined to mix with other children and Anna thought that he cut a lonely figure at times. It didn't help that other members of the settlement rejected him.

He had however developed into a fine young man, despite his strange appearance. At over six feet tall, slender and with a shock of blond hair, he was striking to say the least. But it was his eyes, those huge piercing blue eyes with their unusual pupils that seemed to burn into your soul every time he looked at you, that were the most striking of all. Despite all this Joseph wasn't arrogant, showing patience and great sensitivity with everyone. So when it looked like he was going to break his promise to Marianne, Middlebrook was surprised.

By early evening, just as they had given up hope, Joseph came strolling into camp.

"Mother – father, he's arrived!" exclaimed Marianne excitedly barging into the lodge that they had made for themselves, "come and see, Joseph's here."

Marianne had grown into a fine young woman and was the image of her mother when she was that age.

About five foot six inches tall with long, straight, jet black hair, Marianne had become quite a beauty.

Anna and Middlebrook looked at each other in relief and followed Marianne out into the courtyard. There with a big grin on his face was Joseph, covered in dust and sand but no worse for wear. After Marianne had hugged him and then playfully chastised him for turning up at the eleventh hour, Anna and Middlebrook gave him a hug to welcome him back.

"You cut it a bit fine didn't you?" said Middlebrook.

"I said that I would be back in time," replied Joseph, "did you honestly think I would have broken my promise?"

"No – of course not," said Middlebrook, "it's great to have you home. Come, let's get you some food and drink, you must be starving."

Joseph nodded and followed as they all ambled into the lodge for supper, it was getting late in the day and tomorrow was going to be a busy one.

* * *

"Not much of a turnout is there?" commented Marianne, though not surprised.

It was the afternoon of her and Joseph's birthday party and only a few had turned up.

"I suppose that's because of me." stated Joseph.

"It's not your fault that they are acting like dicks," replied Marianne.

The inhabitants of the settlement were divided in their opinions of Joseph; some were perturbed and found him disturbing. Others embraced him for who he was: a kind, intelligent and thoughtful soul.

The only people who bothered to turn up were Megan and Cristian who also brought their children, Jake and Sara. Ed also came along.

"I'm sorry that we couldn't splash out on food a little more," said Anna walking up to Marianne and Joseph, "it's as much as we could spare. I have made you a fruit cake though but no icing or candles alas."

"It's perfectly fine Mother," replied Marianne, "this is plenty."

Anna moved away and Marianne turned back to Joseph. "Look what Mum and Dad gave me," she said holding up a silver heart shaped locket proudly, "it belonged to her Mum."

Joseph smiled at Marianne's delight though he had no real interest in material things.

"It's a shame that they didn't have anything to give you," she continued.

Joseph shrugged. "No matter," he said, "the best present that I could have had is for Joe to talk to me."

Marianne put a sympathetic hand on his forearm,

"He'll come round," she said, "someday."

"You think?" retorted Joseph unable to hide his misgivings.

"Hey you two," called Middlebrook, "it's time to cut the cake and make a wish."

"Aren't we a bit old for that Dad?" winced Marianne.

"No, you're never too old," encouraged Middlebrook ushering them over to the table.

They cut the cake as the others sang 'Happy Birthday' and then Anna started to pass some cake round to the guests. Joseph was taking his second mouthful when this strange feeling came over him. A feeling of dread, like something terrible was about to happen. The sensation grew more urgent to the point where he put down his plate and dashed out of the lodge.

"Where are you going?" shouted Anna.

"Quick – the field," was all Joseph said and continued running. Alarmed by his behaviour they all followed behind him.

In one the fields next to the settlement stood a large oak tree and high in its branches was a ten-year-old boy reaching out on one of the limbs to try and retrieve a kite which had become entangled. It was Brett, and as he inched further along the branch, it could no longer support his weight and snapped. He plummeted to the ground screaming just as Joseph reached the tree. Joseph caught him but the impact knocked them both to the ground and as they lay there on the grass Brett's mother came rushing up.

"What are you doing?" she screamed hysterically, "leave my son alone you freak."

Everyone stood looking at Molly, the boy's mother, astounded by her reaction.

"But Mum," cried Brett jumping to Joseph's defence, "he saved my life."

"I don't care," she insisted looking round at the group staring at her, "he shouldn't be here. He doesn't belong."

Molly dragged Brett back to her hut and the others returned to the lodge.

"Well that has put a damper on the party," said Joseph as they stepped back inside.

"How did you know?" enquired Marianne.

Joseph shrugged; he didn't fully understand these sensations himself.

Later that evening Marianne looked outside to see Joseph sitting out on the porch. It was a clear evening and the temperature had dropped to below freezing. She put on a coat and went out to join him. Joseph was sitting there with no coat on seemingly staring blankly at the stars.

"Aren't you cold?" asked Marianne with a shiver, sitting down next to him.

"Me? No not at all."

"Don't trouble yourself over that stupid woman," said Marianne trying to be supportive.

"Oh," replied Joseph absentmindedly, "I'd forgotten about that."

Still looking up into the night's sky he continued, "Do you know, it amazes me that with all their technology the Black Eyes chose to look to the past, why didn't they look to the stars? That's where my people will go one day. Not in my lifetime but within the next five hundred years maybe."

"Why did you go away?" asked Marianne.

"I needed to send out a message."

"What do you mean?"

"I needed to find somewhere peaceful where I could meditate," explained Joseph, "I sent out a message to all of my kind. Like a beacon. It's time for us to move. I don't belong here. Molly was right, but for the wrong reasons."

A look of melancholy had descended on Marianne. Joseph put a comforting arm around her and said, "You don't belong here either. There's nothing here for you."

It was true, if Marianne was going to find someone to settle down with she was going to have to move on. It was the same for all the children. Anna and Middlebrook knew it but didn't want to face the fact. They were in their mid-fifties now and were settled. Uprooting to go and find more humans was not something they had envisioned.

"What about your father? You can't go and leave things unresolved," said Marianne.

Joseph acknowledged this fact knowing that it was something that he was going to have to address.

He finally said, "Let's go in, before you get a chill."

* * *

The following day Joseph approached Middlebrook, he wanted to talk to him about his immediate plans.

"I shall be leaving here soon," said Joseph getting straight to the point, "you must have realised that this day would eventually come."

"Yes but not quite so soon."

"While I was away, I sent out an invitation to all of my people on this continent. They will be moving soon and I must meet them."

"How will they escape?" enquired Middlebrook.

"They won't need to escape," laughed Joseph, "they will simply leave. No one can stop them, not even the Black Eyes."

"Where will you meet? Where will you go?"

"We will meet on the edge of what used to be called the Nevada desert," stated Joseph.

Middlebrook paused for thought taking all this in.

"I think you should seriously consider moving the whole camp out," continued Joseph.

"You mean go with you?"

"Not necessarily, but you do need to look for more people of your own kind."

"Why do you say that?"

"Come," smiled Joseph, "as an observer of human nature you must realise that there is no future here for Marianne and the other children. They will need people of their own age, to settle with."

Middlebrook had to admit the sense in what Joseph was saying, but would the rest of the settlement agree to the idea?

"I will have to put the idea forward to the others," said Middlebrook at last, "they must be made to see the wisdom of it."

"Or maybe the intelligence," corrected Joseph, "the two are not the same."

"As I see it, the main hurdle will be convincing them to leave their familiar surroundings for destinations unknown."

"Knowledge doesn't always guarantee certainty, It's a risk that I think you all must take Barnabus."

Middlebrook considered the remarkable young man sitting opposite him.

"You know I can't recall you ever being ill or even poorly," he said eventually, "Marianne came down with the usual ailments but you – you never even caught a cold. Biologically you seem to be perfect."

"Almost perfect," replied Joseph with an impish smile on his face, "I'm not immortal."

"And what of the afterlife, do you believe in that?"

"I believe in the here and now, everything else is pure conjecture."

"So you don't believe the body has a soul then?"

Joseph thought this question through for a moment and then said, "We *are* a soul," he said eventually. "We have a body."

At that moment their conversation was interrupted by Sara, the eleven-year-old daughter of Cristian and Megan.

"Doc, Joseph, come quickly, Joe has collapsed." She was panicking and in tears.

"Where is he?" said Middlebrook with urgency.

"I was helping him feed the chickens and he just collapsed," she sobbed.

They ran over to the chicken coop and found Joe lying flat out on his back with a twisted expression on his face. Middlebrook examined him.

"Help me get him inside; I think he's had a stroke."

By now Ed and Cristian had arrived and soon Joe was laid out on his bed.

"There's nothing we can do for him," said Middlebrook hopelessly, "we just haven't got the medical supplies or equipment to treat him."

Middlebrook suspected that something like this would eventually happen to Joe. He was always living on borrowed time.

"I'm so sorry Joseph; I know you always wanted to reconcile your differences."

"His differences," replied Joseph sullenly, "his differences Barnabus."

Anna came rushing into the hut. "I've just heard," she said, giving Joseph a sympathetic look. She took his arm but Joseph walked past her and out into the courtyard. He needed space to think.

Later that day, Anna, Middlebrook and Marianne were in the lodge getting ready to sit down to supper. A place had been set for Joseph but no one had seen him all day.

"He couldn't have gone far," stated Marianne, "do you think I should go and look for him?"

"Leave him be," said Anna, "he'll come back when he's good and ready."

It was late when Joseph eventually walked in. Anna and Marianne had retired to bed and Middlebrook had decided to wait for Joseph to return.

"At last," said Middlebrook, "we were worried about you."

"There was no need, I can look after myself." Joseph paused deep in thought and then eventually said, "I am going to sit by my father tonight; someone needs to watch over him."

After giving Joseph a hug, Middlebrook retired to bed. Joseph left the lodge and made his way over to Joe's hut. It was time for him to finally confront his father.

Joe, lying on the bed, was in a deep coma, his breathing was shallow and he was barely alive. After finding some blankets Joseph laid them on the floor next to his father. Then he laid down on the blankets and took his father's hand in his. Looking up at the ceiling, Joseph composed himself, closed his eyes and drifted off into a deep meditative state.

* * *

The sun felt warm on Joe's face as he laid there on the sand. He opened his eyes and suddenly sat up in surprise.

"I know this place," he said out loud to himself.

The view in front of him was of a beautiful beach, with the sea sparkling in the sunlight and gently rushing up the sand. Beyond the beach, jagged rocks gave a good level of seclusion, framing the small cove and tapering off into the sea.

"I found it deep in your subconscious," said Joseph who was sitting next to him.

"I came here once as a child," said Joe, "I'd almost forgotten it."

Joe's expression suddenly turned from one of wonder to confusion.

"How did we get here?"

"Please don't alarm yourself father," said Joseph, anxious to placate his fears. "You haven't long, I have joined with you to say goodbye."

"Then I'm not really here then?"

Joseph shook his head. "Not really no, but isn't that what memories are for; to relive those moments?"

Joe looked at his son, suddenly ridden with guilt for the way that he had treated him. All bitterness and resentment towards him seemed to have vanished.

"I'm so sorry Joseph," said Joe with great sincerity, "I was wrong to treat you the way I did. I failed you. Can you ever forgive me?"

"Of course, that's why I'm here,"

Joe and Joseph hugged each other tightly and were suddenly distracted by a voice.

"Hello Joe."

The voice came from the other side of the beach. Two figures were glowing so brightly that both of them had to shield their eyes. Eventually they were able to discern the people standing there. It was Alice and Katlin smiling at both of them, their bodies shimmering with luminescence.

"Who is that?" asked Joseph.

"The one on the right is your mother," replied Joe in wonder.

Then a third figure moved forward between Alice and Katlin. It was Isobel, Joe's wife. She held a hand up to beckon to him.

"It's time to go now Joe," she said with a kindly reassuring smile.

"Where are we going?"

"We're taking you home," said Isobel simply.

Joe got to his feet and Joseph stood up also. He turned to Joseph and said, "Goodbye son."

Joe hugged him again and then started to walk over to the girls. Joe was glowing like them now and Joseph had to cover his eyes. As he reached them Alice looked over to Joseph with a smile and waved.

Everything suddenly went black and Joseph came to, violently sitting bolt upright as if he had been punched in the stomach. He gave out a gasp of air and sat there panting for a few moments. His father's hand was hanging limply from the side of the bed and it was obvious to Joseph that his father had passed on.

Joseph decided to stay there with his father until eventually, dawn started to break.

As the sun rose higher, Anna and Middlebrook looked in to see a forlorn Joseph sitting by the bed.

"He's gone," said Joseph, "he is at peace now."

Later that day, a grave was dug close to the large oak tree in one of the fields. Everyone at the settlement attended the funeral, putting aside any differences and animosity they had towards Joseph, at least for the moment. The death of Joe brought home the fragile existence that they were living and Middlebrook felt the urgency to move on more than ever. Joseph was right.

* * *

A meeting was held the next day and Middlebrook put forward the idea of leaving to find more people or larger settlements.

"I see the logic in what you're suggesting," said Leo the father of Brett, "but there's no guarantee that we'll find anybody. It's too much of a risk."

"Look if we stay here there's nothing for our children," replied Middlebrook. "Think of Brett, he will need more than this when he matures."

The meeting very quickly descended into those who agreed and those who didn't.

"Look," shouted Middlebrook eventually, "my family will be moving out at the end of the week. Those who want to come with us come and see us at the lodge." With that he walked out and the meeting dispersed.

"Do you think any of them will come?" enquired Marianne.

"We will have to wait and see," said Anna hopefully.

It wasn't long before someone was knocking on their door. Cristian, Megan and their two children, Jake and Sara, stood there smiling as Anna opened it.

"We've decided to come with you," said Megan.

"What about the others?" enquired Middlebrook.

Cristian shook his head. "I'm afraid we're the only ones."

The rest of the day was spent planning their journey, deciding what to take with them and what to leave behind.

"We'll take one of the trucks," said Middlebrook, "there will be eight of us travelling. And we will need extra fuel; our first stop will be the edge of the Nevada desert."

"But that's about seven hundred miles away!" exclaimed Cristian.

"I know but Joseph has a rendezvous there so it cannot be helped."

The others looked at Joseph, who stared back apologetically and said nothing.

"We'll start organising things tomorrow," said Cristian standing up.

"Good enough," replied Middlebrook, "til tomorrow then."

After announcing their intentions, Middlebrook and his family started to get everything they needed for the journey.

"Only pack essentials," said Middlebrook, "space will be tight in the truck."

It had been a busy day, unusually warm for February, and by the afternoon they decided to sit on the porch and eat some lunch. Suddenly, as if out of nowhere, a figure sauntered casually into the settlement.

* * *

The figure was female, tall and slender with blonde spikey elfin styled hair. Her eyes were blue and huge like Joseph's and he sat there with his jaw wide open, a fork of food poised at his mouth.

Middlebrook walked down to confront the girl.

"Please forgive me but I think that I might be lost," she said.

"Where have you come from?" enquired Middlebrook.

"I don't know exactly," the girl replied, "I have been travelling for a few days since I heard the call."

By now Joseph had got his wits together and approached them,

"I'm very pleased to see you," was the best that he could think of at that moment, "it was me, I sent out the call."

Joseph couldn't help staring at the girl; she was the most beautiful creature he had ever seen. The girl stared back smiling at him and Middlebrook started to feel awkward – a spare part in the conversation.

"What's your name?" Middlebrook asked to cover his unease.

"I haven't got a name," replied the girl, "just this number."

She pointed to the left-hand side of her dress, just below her shoulder where a six digit serial number had been embroidered.

Middlebrook and Joseph looked at each other appalled but not surprised.

"You must be tired and hungry," said Joseph, "come, we have plenty."

The girl smiled again and thanked them. As they sat back down to eat, Joseph turned to the girl and said, "The first thing we do tomorrow is get you to choose a name for yourself."

The girl simply nodded and tucked into her food, she was hungry.

CHAPTER THIRTEEN
EXODUS – CHAPTER 41

On the day they were going to leave, Joseph was sat in a chair on the porch looking over the settlement. The sky was partially cloudy and there was a nip in the air. Joseph didn't notice it however, he was deep in thought.

"Have you been out here all night?" enquired Marianne pretending to be cross with him as she walked out on to the porch.

"I was talking to the new girl for most of the night, do you know the Black Eyes treated her like a slave. Imagine: her with an intellect of infinite potency and they conduct themselves in such an abhorrent manner."

"But that's the Black Eyes in a nutshell, isn't it," said Marianne, "they have no respect for life. It makes you wonder why they bothered to breed your race at all."

"What is she doing now?" enquired Joseph.

"Dad's got her looking through his book collection."

"What for?"

"To pick a name, silly. You can't call her the new girl forever."

"Oh," replied Joseph feeling a little foolish, "of course. I've been a little distracted this morning."

"What is it?" asked Marianne, she could see that he wasn't his normal self. Perhaps he was just tired from being up all night.

"I've been thinking about my mother," said Joseph eventually. Then after a long pause he asked, "What is your earliest memory?"

Marianne had to think about this for a few seconds. "I don't know," then she said, "I suppose it must be when I was about two. I remember falling on a flint and cutting my knee open. I still have a scar where it healed up. What about you?"

"I have this vague memory of communicating with my mother. I sensed her anxiety and wanted to alleviate it. This vision of a door opening keeps cropping up in my head and the sense of anxiety seemed to dissipate quickly."

"Perhaps it was a dream that you once had and now you perceive it as a memory," suggested Marianne.

"That's unlikely, I rarely dream."

"Are you two coming in for some breakfast?" It was Anna who was trying to get everyone organised for their departure.

"Yes Mother," said Marianne rolling her eyes impatiently. She gave Joseph a sympathetic glance and took his hand then both of them walked inside to eat.

As they sat down at the table the new girl, known only as a number, was pouring over one of Middlebrooks's books.

"Have you had any ideas on a name?" enquired Marianne.

"Yes I have," said the girl looking up from the book, "I rather like the name Mary."

"You can't call yourself that!" exclaimed Joseph choking on his drink, "what book have you got there?"

The girl lifted up the book to reveal the black cover and on the front in gold lettering it said *The Holy Bible*.

"Why not?" said the girl feeling a little indignant, "it's a nice name and I like it."

"But it's Joseph and Mary," stated an exasperated Joseph.

"I know – so what?" she retorted with a mischievous look on her face, "besides what makes you think that we are going to pair off?"

Joseph had to admit that he had kind of taken the fact for granted. After all there had been a mutual attraction between them from the moment they met. For once he was lost for words.

"Barnabus," called Joseph eventually, "have you heard the name that she has decided on?"

"Mary has decided on," teased Marianne with a big grin on her face.

Middlebrook walked into the room smiling.

"Yes – she suggested it to me earlier, It could've been worse though, her first choice was Deliah."

Shaking his head in defeat Joseph got up from the table to get some breakfast, he looked at Middlebrook in despair and said, "Of all the books she could have chosen, it had to be that one."

* * *

As the light began to fade later that day, Middlebrook and the rest of his party were saying their farewells to the group who were staying. Joseph and Mary held back and stood by the truck which they would be leaving in.

Sensing Joseph's sadness at never having been fully accepted, she took his hand and said,

"You needn't be sad, let them have their moment, Homo Sapiens haven't got long on this planet, their time is over. It is us the Neo Sapiens who will take this world into a new age."

"Neo Sapiens," said Joseph perking up, "I like that."

"Their whole evolutionary existence has compelled them to fear and distrust anything different. All of their history has been plagued by war, mostly for this reason."

"I feel sorry for Barnabus and his family," mused Joseph, "they are good people, they do not deserve this fate."

By now Middlebrook and the others were walking back to the truck.

"Okay," he said, "let's see if we can get this thing started." He climbed aboard the truck and turned the key in the ignition. The engine gave a slow whining groan and gave up. "The batteries dead," said Middlebrook jumping out of the truck.

"What are we going to do now?" asked Anna, "we have no means to charge it back up again."

Dispirited at this turn of events Cristian said, "Did no one think to check it?"

"What's the problem?" enquired Joseph, "maybe I can help."

"I don't think so Joseph. Not this time," replied Middlebrook.

"Show me," insisted Joseph.

Middlebrook opened the bonnet of the truck and pointed at the battery.

"There's no power in this battery," he said and started to close the bonnet again, "we're stuck."

"Wait," said Joseph, "get back in and when I say 'go' you turn the key."

Confused, Middlebrook climbed back into the cabin and waited on Joseph's instruction, having no idea what he was going to do. Joseph placed a hand on each terminal, gripped tightly and closed his eyes. A few seconds later with a screwed up look of concentration on his face Joseph shouted, "Go!"

Middlebrook turned the key and the truck's engine sprang into life. Joseph pulled his hands off of the terminals as if he had been touching something very hot and gently blew on them.

"How the hell did you do that?" asked an incredulous Middlebrook.

"I concentrated the electrical impulses in my body down my arms that's all," Joseph replied, in a way that suggested anyone could do it.

"'That's all' he says. Is there no end to your talents?"

Joseph just smiled and shrugged. "I will only know the answer to that at the end of my life."

With the truck's engine still ticking over, they all climbed in with Middlebrook in the driving seat and Cristian riding shotgun.

"I want to make this journey in one continuous stint," said Middlebrook, "the quicker that we get to Nevada, the less chance we'll have of running into trouble. We'll drive in shifts."

"Do you really think Joseph's people will be waiting for him there?" enquired a sceptical Cristian.

"If Joseph says they will be there, then I believe him," stated Middlebrook.

After twenty-one years, he knew better than to doubt anything Joseph said or did. He put the truck into gear, released the handbrake and pulled away. The remainder of the settlement walked to the entrance waving as they left and watched as the truck eventually disappeared into the distance.

* * *

Darkness fell quickly and Middlebrook decided to take full advantage of the cover of night to make as much progress as possible.

The truck travelled west through the evening making as much use of the roads that were left. By dawn they had travelled over five hundred miles. Space was tight in the back and made sleeping difficult but everyone made do the best they could.

"Do you think it would be safe to stop and switch off the engine?" asked Cristian. He had taken over driving duties in the small hours of the morning.

Middlebrook considered this, "Let's find a secluded spot and find out, the battery should be charged a good bit and I think we could all do with stretching our legs."

A short while later Cristian pulled off of the road and drove down a track which led to some trees. Finally, he parked up and everyone got out. Immediately the women set to making breakfast. Joseph stood eating and looking westward

"We are very close," he said, "I can feel their presence, it's really strong now."

"Hopefully we will reach the desert by the end of day," stated Middlebrook.

"If it's alright with you, I would like to ride upfront," asked Joseph.

"Of course," smiled Middlebrook, "I'm sure Cristian won't mind."

Presently they were back on the road again, only now Middlebrook, who was back in the driving seat, felt it prudent to keep off of the main roads.

"We won't make such good time," he commented, "I would guess that we have about two to three hundred miles to go. Hopefully we will make our, or at least your, rendezvous point just before dusk."

As they travelled the countryside, Joseph took the opportunity to enjoy the view from the vantage point of the cabin. With nearly all evidence of human activity being wiped out by the Black Eyes, the twenty-one years since Joseph's birth had allowed the planet to revert to a condition that displayed little human intervention and was all the better for it. Forests had expanded, meadows with wild flowers had returned to strength and this had an impact on insect recovery. In fact the whole eco system had recovered to a point before human overpopulation.

"It's still a beautiful planet," said Middlebrook enjoying the vista. "It's hard to believe we've recently endured something akin to an Armageddon."

"Armageddon for the Human Race," commented Joseph, "not the planet."

"I sometimes think that you don't like us very much," said Middlebrook.

"I feel that you have let yourselves down badly in the past."

"In what way?"

"If you ignore the constant bickering," continued Joseph, "there is the matter of how you have treated the planet. This place is your home and you have been slowly but methodically destroying it. And for what? Nearly all human activity is motivated by greed, leaving the problems created, for future generations to deal with. The Black Eyes have inadvertently done the planet a favour. By decimating the human population they have allowed the Earth to recover from man's profanation."

"Profanation," blurted Middlebrook, feeling that Joseph's words were a little harsh, "do you think your race will be any better?"

"We are not motivated by greed, the planet does not belong to us. It is only on loan from future generations and it is our responsibility to take care of it for them. The problem is," he continued, "humans do not live long enough. With a life span of about eighty years, they have a tendency to think 'It will never happen in my lifetime' so as a result no one worries about the damage that they are doing. If you all lived to, say, one hundred and fifty or longer, I'm sure that you would think twice about what you are doing to the planet."

It was difficult to argue with Joseph so Middlebrook fell silent and got on with the task of reaching their destination as soon as possible.

In the back of the truck Mary sat studying Marianne opposite her. "You are sad," she said, perceiving her emotions.

Marianne nodded glumly, she had been thinking ahead to when they and Joseph part company. "I'm going to miss Joseph."

"You were very close?"

"We grew up together. He is my brother and best friend. It is hard to imagine him not being around."

"Do not worry," said Mary with a kindly smile, "I will take good care of him."

For the rest of the day the truck continued on, passing through Utah and The Great Salt Lake until eventually by late afternoon they finally crossed the border into Nevada.

As the desert loomed into view, suddenly Joseph and Middlebrook noticed what looked like a massive make-shift campsite. The truck pulled to a halt on the edge of the site and Joseph jumped out and ran to the back, eager for Mary to see the site.

"Mary come quick, you've got to see this."

After they had all scrambled out of the back, Mary stood beside Joseph and together they beheld the sight in front of them.

"Look," he said excitedly, "thousands and thousands of them, just like us."

The occupants of the site had heard the truck arrive and were now walking slowly towards it with caution and curiosity.

"Why are you so surprised?" said Mary, "your signal was a powerful message to unify. We all felt it, and this is the result."

Joseph and Mary walked over to the crowd now getting close to them and mingled with their own kind greeting, talking and laughing.

"We won't see them for a while," said Anna.

"Can you blame them," observed Middlebrook, "for the first time in their lives they probably feel like they belong somewhere."

By nightfall, Middlebrook and his group had set up a camp for the night and cooked a meal. Eventually Joseph and Mary came back to talk to them.

"I'm sorry that we just took off and left you," said Joseph.

"That's quite alright," replied Anna, "we understand."

"What are your plans now?" enquired Marianne.

"It has been decided to assemble very soon and make our way across the desert, with the intention of settling in what was once called California."

"That's quite a hike," stated Middlebrook, "you're sure that you can make it?"

"Yes – quite sure," insisted Joseph, "we are tougher than we look."

"We shall be returning to our people soon," said Mary. "We have much to discuss."

"As have we," concurred Middlebrook, "we will see you in the morning."

Joseph and Mary stood up and smiled at the group sitting round their camp fire and then walked away back to their encampment.

* * *

As the sun rose the following morning, Joseph returned again to the truck. He approached the group and after accepting a cup of coffee, sat down to speak to them.

"Have you decided what your next move will be?"

"We thought perhaps of heading south," replied Middlebrook.

Joseph nodded. "Talking to some of my people last night, they told me that on their way here they were quite sure that they passed some human settlements; a large settlement to the south."

"Did they give any indication how far?" enquired Anna.

"Maybe three, four hundred miles away."

"That's what we will do then," said Middlebrook decisively, "we should just have enough fuel left to get there."

At that moment a dull roar could be heard coming from the east and they all looked in that direction alerted by the sound.

Middlebrook, Joseph and Cristian moved away from the truck to a clearer area to get a better view of the source of the sound. In the distance they could just about make out ten large craft flying towards them at speed getting ever larger in the heat haze.

"I don't like the look of this," said Middlebrook with a frown."

By now the rest of the group was watching anxiously as the ten craft loomed closer.

"It's got to be Black Eyes," said Cristian.

Soon the craft were almost on top of them, stopping suddenly two hundred yards away and hovering. The vessels were boxy in shape, dark grey in colour and very large. Then from their rear appeared a much smaller gold coloured vessel, much sleeker than the others. This smaller vessel took formation in front, hovered for a few seconds and then they all gently landed on the ground, billowing clouds of sand up into the air as they did so.

"This is not good," said Marianne, "what on earth do they want?"

"I think we are about to find out," added Middlebrook sardonically.

At that moment doors to the sides of the large grey vessels opened and hundreds of Nih-troopers poured out and formed orderly lines in front of their craft. A hatch opened on the smaller golden vessel and ten Nih-troopers marched out followed by another Deviant in a grey uniform with insignia picked out in red on his sleeves. He walked to the centre of the landing party and stood there with his ten guards close behind him. It was DM

Khai Drypha standing with his legs slightly apart and his arms folded.

"Who in God's name is that!" exclaimed Cristian.

Joseph, who had noticed his people assembling behind him, walked across and held a hand out to command them to halt.

"What shall we do?" enquired Middlebrook for the first time at a loss.

"It's time to introduce myself," announced Joseph.

With that he started to walk across the sand and stopped fifty feet away from the Deviant in the grey uniform.

"Greetings," said Drypha with a bow and a menacing grin, "please allow me to introduce myself: DM. Khai Drypha, Commander-In-Chief."

"My name is Joseph Denham." Joseph had taken his mother's surname since Joe had disowned him until the very end of his life.

Drypha looked genuinely surprised, "Alice's child. I always wondered what became of you. You've grown into a fine young man."

"What do you want Drypha?" asked Joseph not wanting to engage in small talk.

Drypha's expression suddenly turned serious as much because of the lack of respect he was being shown by this young upstart.

"Come now," he said, trying to maintain his composure, "we have been following you for some time. We were curious to know of your intent. After all our effort and planning, did you honestly think that we could just allow you all walk away from us?"

"There's nothing you can do to stop us," stated Joseph calmly.

"I have over five hundred troops and enough fire power to destroy you all," Drypha sneered.

"And yet it isn't enough," smiled Joseph, "you are weakened, a shadow of what you used to be. The moment that you violated this era," he continued, "you were racing headlong down a dead end to your own extinction. You are an evolutionary anachronism, destined to simply fade away into historical indifference. Posterity has already abandoned you."

"So do you think you are better than us?" shouted Drypha bristling with anger. "You are nothing but mongrels."

"Mongrels, crossbreeds or even biological chimera," sneered Joseph, "what does it matter if the outcome is a good one. We are not abominations like you and your kind. Unlike you and the human race before you, we will cherish this planet."

"The time for talking is over," said Drypha calmly, and motioned with his arms for troops to assemble beside him – fifty either side. There was a stand-off for a minute with both sides staring at each other.

"Please don't do this," pleaded Joseph, "no good can come from it."

A low drone had started behind Joseph coming from the thousands of his people who had gathered a short distance away from him.

"Kill him!" said Drypha casually to the hundred troopers.

They raised their laser guns as the drone became more intense. Joseph closed his eyes and concentrated. The collective power of thousands of minds was brought to bear and the Nih-troopers started to shake as if fighting against something which had taken over their will. They started to move in some kind of grotesque choreography until they had formed a circle with Drypha at the centre.

"I said kill him!" shouted Drypha, confused and panicking. He spun round looking at his troops, their laser guns were all trained on him. Drypha put his hands up to his ears the drone was becoming too intense to bare.

Fire, thought Joseph with his eyes still closed.

In that instant one hundred powerful laser beams hit Drypha on all sides. The air heated up and expanded in his lungs, the moisture burst out from his eyes and the blood in his veins boiled, then with a final gut wrenching scream his body exploded. Flesh, blood and body parts flew in all directions.

Middlebrook and his group looked on horrified at this sight but could not look away. The drone continued and the Nih-troopers with their laser guns still trained on each other were commanded to fire again. Most of the beams hit their mark and only seven troopers were left standing.

Joseph took a few steps towards them and immediately they put their weapons down and started to back off. Then the golden vessel rose into the air and shot a laser directly at Joseph. He braced himself for the impact, held out his right arm with the palm of his hand upright ready to deflect the assault. The beam hit his hand and shot back at great speed hitting Drypha's craft and causing it to blow apart. The vessel dropped to the ground in flames and Joseph turned his attention to the remaining Nih-troopers.

"Bear witness to what has taken place here today, and tell the rest of your people to leave us alone, or they can expect the same fate."

The droning had subsided by now and a tense calm fell on the scene. Silently the troopers dispersed and steadily re-embarked their craft. Eventually they rose into the air causing a cloud of dust to blow over Joseph who was still standing, rooted to the spot. He closed his eyes to shield them from the dust as the vessels turned around and fled back in the direction in which they had come.

Joseph stood there now alone, he opened his eyes turned around and walked back to the expectant multitude. They surrounded him cheering and congratulating him as though welcoming home a conquering hero.

"He's quite frightening," said Middlebrook, awe struck. "I hope Joseph has the wisdom to realise that great power brings great responsibility."

"I'm just glad that he's on our side," commented Anna.

"I never ever thought he was capable of killing," said Marianne. She was clearly shaken.

As Joseph disappeared into the crowd, Middlebrook and his group returned to their camp still dazed from what they had just witnessed.

* * *

"I'm sorry you had to see that." said Joseph, when he eventually returned to Middlebrook and the others," "but I had no choice."

"You've crossed the Rubicon," said Middlebrook sadly, "I never imagined that you might kill."

"What was I to do? Barnabus," uttered Joseph, "let them destroy us all?"

"I don't know," he replied, "you know how I feel about violence. It rarely solves anything."

"This is the first time," stated Joseph. "I am hoping it will also be the last. The Black Eyes underestimated our power."

Middlebrook nodded, it was true. For all their intelligence and ingenuity, the Deviants' ultimate weakness was arrogance and conceit.

"Hubris will get you every time," he said finally.

"When will you be moving out?" enquired Marianne.

"Very soon; everyone is packing up ready for the march, I have returned to say goodbye."

"I shall miss you," said Marianne with tears in her eyes, "I don't suppose we will see each other again."

"No I don't believe we will," agreed Joseph with genuine emotion in his voice.

One by one he hugged them all, finally leaving Middlebrook, Anna and Marianne until last.

"You two have been both mother and father to me," said Joseph, "I will be forever in your debt."

"Take good care of yourself – and Mary," said Anna.

"Live a good life," said Middlebrook putting his disappointment in Joseph to one side.

Finally, Joseph turned to Marianne who by now had given up trying to control her emotions. Tears were streaming down her face.

"Marianne, you have been my sister, friend and confidante for all of our lives. Words cannot describe how much I will miss you."

After one more lingering look, Joseph smiled and departed.

They all watched sullenly as Joseph took his place at the front of the crowd and slowly the multitude began to move off. A cloud of dust could be seen for miles as thousands of feet kicked up the sand until eventually they could see them no more. The dust finally settled and the remaining group were all alone.

"Well we'd better see if we can get this truck moving," said Cristian.

"Okay you two," said Megan to Jake and Sara, "help me to pack these things away."

"I'm scared Mum. What will become of us?" said Marianne helping her mother to load up the truck.

"It's just fear of the unknown," reassured Anna, "that will never change."

In no time at all they were ready to leave and Cristian jumped up into the driver's seat with Middlebrook beside him. He put the key in the ignition and looked at Middlebrook apprehensively. Then he turned it and the truck roared into life almost immediately. They both laughed in relief, half expecting the battery to be dead.

"I feel like the old pioneers riding off into the unknown," said Cristian.

"That's exactly what we are, let's hope there's something out there for us," hoped Middlebrook, studying a compass and then pointing in their direction of travel. "We need to head that way."

Cristian put the truck into gear and they moved off in a southerly direction, hoping to find what might be left of the Human Race.

Epilogue

On the day after Joseph's 295th birthday, he had asked to be taken to his favourite dwelling place: the domicile that he had built for himself on the peak of Mount Diablo. From here he had a panoramic view of New San Frisco, the bay and the Pacific Ocean beyond. The metropolis he oversaw the construction of decades ago, was quite a sight and he could not help but feel proud of all that had been achieved. Cities like this had sprung up all over the globe, and he realised that this must be the longest period of complete world peace since any sentient being walked this earth. No single person ruled in their society and nobody went hungry. It was as close to utopia as any civilisation could be.

Joseph recalled Middlebrook once asking him whether Neo Sapiens would be any better and this just confirmed his belief that they were.

Thinking of Middlebrook and the others, Joseph hoped they had had a long and contented life, knowing full well that humans lacked a certain propensity for contentment. He rather suspected that this foolish race had probably bickered with itself rather like spoilt children. As humans had not been seen for over a hundred years now, or Black Eyes for that matter, he reasonably assumed that they had the planet to themselves.

Eighty years earlier an expedition was sent out to reconnoitre further inland and a number of human settlements were discovered. Joseph watched via a live video feed as each settlement was shown to be dilapidated and devoid of all human activity. During a video from one of the larger settlements, his heart jumped into his mouth as he saw the truck which he arrived at the Nevada desert in, standing there derelict and rusting; it's markings unmistakable. Outside the settlement was a cemetery with several graves, alas all unmarked. Joseph could only speculate as to what might have happened to them all; he had said goodbye to Barnabus, Anna, Marianne and the others over two hundred years earlier, so if anyone had survived it would have been their descendants.

Two Deviant bases were also found, but these were deserted and dilapidated as well, save for a few abandoned corpses that had decayed to skeletons. The exploration party suspected that they probably turned on each other and finally resorted to cannibalism. Nature had taken over as ivy and creepers were covering the outside walls. The giant spheres had sunk into the ground with trees and shrubs growing up to partially obscure them.

The last fifty years had been lonely for Joseph, ever since Mary had passed away, and he was beginning to feel tired himself now. Between them they had four children, a dozen grandchildren, and he had given up trying to remember how many great-grandchildren and great-great-grandchildren they had. It was quite a dynasty and Joseph felt it was time to pass the torch to his eldest son Viraj, before he joined his wife. First though there was one last thing he had to do.

Joseph walked over to the videocom and contacted his eldest daughter Feezah.

"Hello father," she said, slightly surprised to be hearing from him so late.

Feezah couldn't help but notice how old her father looked and wondered sadly how much time he had left.

"I want you and Viraj to come up to the lodge and bring some cutting tools with you. When can you depart?"

"We could probably bring them tomorrow; I'll have to check that Viraj isn't busy first though."

Feezah was puzzled by this request. *What can the old man be up to now?* she thought.

"That will be fine," said Joseph, "let me know if you can't make it. Oh and bring Metra and Atiki with you as well."

They finished the call and Joseph walked out onto the balcony of his mountain lodge to enjoy the view of the city below and its illuminations. It was starting to get dark and the lights of small vessels buzzing silently through the sky could be seen going about their business. Suddenly feeling the cold, Joseph shuffled back inside and decided to retire for the night. The birthday festivities had taken a lot out him and he welcomed the rest and solitude.

* * *

The following morning Joseph was woken up by a vessel hovering over the landing pad and slowly making its descent. He got up, put on a gown and walked out to greet his children. Viraj and Feezah walked in to look for their father whilst the other younger siblings Metra and Atiki, brother and sister respectfully, unloaded the equipment that Joseph had requested.

"What do you want it for?" enquired Feezah.

"You will find out soon enough," replied Joseph enigmatically.

After getting dressed and breakfasting with his children, Joseph leaned back and observed them. They had all grown into fine adults and he was extremely proud of them. His heart was full of sadness however because he knew that this would be the last time he would see them.

"I am old and tired now and ready to join your mother," he said finally.

His children tried to protest but Joseph raised his hand to quell them. "I want you to return here again only after I have gone."

"How will we know?" asked Viraj, not unreasonably.

"Look to these hills," replied Joseph, "you will know when it is time."

They spent the day with their father until eventually it was time to go. He hugged them all in turn and finally said, "Do not despair, I know what awaits me and it is nothing to fear."

Joseph watched as their vessel took off and flew back to the city below. Then he retired to bed; there would be much for him to do tomorrow.

The following morning was full of sunshine and Joseph woke up early. He washed, dressed and ate a light breakfast, then he walked out onto his balcony and shivered, he noticed that he was feeling the cold more and more these days.

Eventually he found the cutting equipment and wheeled it to the rock face that he had chosen. After setting up the laser he began to cut a slice of rock from the mountain to leave a smooth, flat, vertical face.

The magenta coloured laser beam cut through the rock like butter and Joseph watched with satisfaction as a large chunk of rock fell away and broke in two on the ground. The rest of the morning he spent clearing away the discarded rock and then Joseph stopped for lunch.

In the afternoon Joseph set up another piece of equipment facing the rock. He opened up the box-like apparatus to reveal a keyboard and screen. Then Joseph started to type, changing the wording and rearranging it until he was happy with the result. Then he pressed a button and a laser beam cut the wording into the flat rock surface, exactly as it had been displayed on the screen. Finally, Joseph looked at his efforts and smiled. It was a good job.

By evening the old man was very tired; he skipped supper and made his way to bed. Sleep would come quickly this evening and he welcomed it. Joseph laid himself down on his bed and closed his large blue eyes. He didn't expect them to behold this world again.

A whole day had passed since they had left Joseph on the mountain, when his children were woken in the small hours of the morning by a strange sensation. They all instinctively looked outside in the direction of the mountain.

Suddenly they witnessed a powerful beam of white light shoot up into the night sky, it hung there for a moment and then the beam disappeared as suddenly as it had appeared. Viraj contacted the others for a conference call.

"Did you see that?" he asked them.

They all nodded, it was impossible to miss.

"What does it mean?" enquired Atiki.

"I don't know," replied Feezah, "but I think that we should get up there as soon as we can."

By the time they arrived on Joseph's landing pad the sun was just showing over the hill top. They hastily made their way into the lodge. Feezah called to her father but got no reply. Eventually they all entered the bedroom but all they found was a dishevelled bed with a burn mark on the sheets; the outline of Joseph's body.

"What on earth happened here!" exclaimed an alarmed Metra.

"He's gone," said Feezah simply, "he's with mother now."

They knew that his time was close but couldn't help feeling grief-stricken.

Walking out into the mountain air to look for any evidence of what their father might have wanted the cutting equipment for, they eventually they came upon the rock face and read the inscription carved into it. The four siblings looked at each other and said nothing.

The inscription read: '*In Memoriam of Alice Denham Saviour of Mother Earth.*'

It was a fitting tribute to a brave young woman who quite literally battled her demons and won.

The End

Author's Note

Choosing the name St. Clare's for the psychiatric hospital was not a random decision on my part. Many hospitals are named after saints and I wanted to continue this tradition. After researching saint's names and their meanings, my attention was drawn to St. Clare of Assisi.

She was an Italian saint who lived in the first half of the thirteenth century and was one of the first followers of St. Francis of Assisi. Despite coming from a wealthy family, Clare often gave food to the poor and inspired by St. Francis, co-founded the Poor Ladies of San Damiano with her sister Agnes. She lived a rigorously devoted life of prayer, penance and service, continuously caring for her sisters, particularly the weak and all those in need. Later in life when she was too ill to attend Mass, she claimed God had brought Mass to her by displaying it on the wall like a movie, and as a consequence in 1958, she was made the patron saint of television.

The parallels between Clare's vision and Alice's made the use of her name impossible for me to resist. After all, in her own way Clare broke the fourth wall as well.